UNRESTRAINED

A Paranormal, Psychological Thriller

Now committed to a psychiatric hospital, Maggie McGee's only hope for help comes from Ethel, a seer. But will Ethel believe the psychiatrist's diagnosis? Will she be able to stop the evil spirits? Or will she become a victim herself?

(Book 2) Committed to a psychiatric hospital for psychosis, Maggie McGee has lost contact with reality. Spirits from the past have completed the task of leaving her in a living hell, allowing the dark-robed demon to feed on her for the rest of her life. But Maggie has Ethel, a seer, working on her behalf. Will Ethel be able to fight the evil forces without losing her mind? Will she be able to convince Detective Becker to believe her unbelievable story of ghosts, or will he consider her mentally unstable? Will Ethel listen to the psychiatrist and trust his diagnosis that Maggie has a mental disorder brought on by her husband's death, and not by entities? Or is the murderer someone else?

Follow along as parasitic beings continue to smother Maggie, relentlessly pursue Ethel and whoever may be in the way of their promised existence of ecstasy.

ConnieMyres.com

UNRESTRAINED

A Paranormal Psychological Thriller

by

CONNIE MYRES

Feather and Fermion Publishing - Michigan

Dedicated to my family and friends, especially my sons Lucas and Charles Kraus for their loyal support and encouragement of all my projects. I appreciate you.

No amount of sage can cleanse this evil.

1

A RASPY MALE voice from the PA system's loudspeakers, preceded by a harsh, breathy exhale, echoed through the hallways and rooms of the locked unit at the Port Glenn Psychiatric and Forensic Hospital. "Time to get up, everybody." Then he blew into the mic again, "Time to get up."

Maggie rolled on her side and opened her eyes. Being at the mental hospital almost three months, did not make the sight of the white painted brick walls and the open steel door with its small window any less intimidating. Then the realization of the upcoming court hearing flashed into her mind; she wanted to go back to sleep so that she would not have to think about it.

Her heart raced as anxiety about the possibility of being found guilty of murdering her landlord, Mr. Zimmerman, loomed over her. Her friend, Ethel, a seer, was trying to help her by casting spells to keep the black hooded demon away from her. Maggie could feel it feed on her while she slept—when she could sleep—it kept her drained of energy and hope.

Ethel had warned her that the dark entity fed on hopelessness, anger, and despair; but Maggie could not help herself. Her life was a nightmare and she saw no way out.

She sat up on the side of the bed, hunched over in grief. Grief from losing her husband, Cory, to suicide, and grief to being accused of a murder she did not commit. However, convincing anyone that it was a ghost named Susie that was the murderer was pointless, no one, except Ethel, believed her.

It was Saturday, Ethel would be visiting her that afternoon, and Maggie would find out if Ethel had made any progress with Detective John Becker.

She rubbed the side of her aching neck. She felt the same two pea-sized lumps underneath the skin that had first appeared when she was jailed. When she had asked the doctor about them, he said they were just swollen lymph nodes and nothing to worry about.

Maggie slipped on the white sneakers the facility had provided her and fastened the Velcro straps. She walked to her empty desk, picked up the plastic comb and ran it through her snarly hair. Aside from the small black comb, all she had on the desk was a cheap toothbrush, a tiny tube of toothpaste, and hair and body wash.

The tiny-toothed comb seemed to tighten the knots of her tangled locks rather than loosen them. She wanted to give up on combing her hair but since Ethel would likely be visiting, she would try to look at least somewhat presentable. But that did not include taking a shower, she had no energy for that task. Besides, she was only required to shower three days a week anyway.

Maggie believed what Ethel had told her about the black-robed entity. That it was the type of vampire that fed on the energy and life essence of people, leaving them feeling exhausted and unfocused. Psychic parasitism, Ethel called it.

She looked at the small tube of toothpaste and the toothbrush sitting next to the comb, almost deciding not to brush her teeth. Nevertheless, she picked them up and walked down the hallway, past a dozen other patient rooms, to the bathroom. The worker guarding the upstairs sleeping area sat at the top of the stairwell. The stocky middle-aged woman dressed in jeans and a T-shirt stayed focused on her tablet, not bothering to acknowledge Maggie when she walked past. The guard would continue to stare at the tablet in her hands until twenty minutes had passed and it was time to walk down the hallway and check the residents.

Maggie went into the bathroom and examined her neck in the mirror. There were no visible marks, as one would expect to see with a vampire that sucked blood. Then she looked at her tired face. The green sweatshirt and sweatpants—courtesy of the facility—made her look shabby. She shook her head and whispered to herself, "Maggie, you're a sorrowful case."

When she was finished in the bathroom, she returned the items to her room and closed the door before going downstairs to the dayroom. Soon all the doors would be locked and no one would be allowed back upstairs until naptime, later in the afternoon.

Maggie walked past three guards seated at a table in the main room at the bottom of the steps. She sat in one of the chairs lined up and facing the television set. There were no couches or recliners, only cushioned chairs like those that could be found in a doctor's waiting room. She was not interested in the news program playing on TV, but there was nothing else to do until breakfast.

A tall woman in jeans sat down next to her. "How are you today?"

Maggie was not up to talking to another patient, but Chloe liked her and was always following her around and talking to her. "I'm fine, just tired."

"Yeah, the drugs they give us around here make us tired," Chloe said, crossing her legs. Her foot began to bounce with a nervous tick. "They like to keep us subdued."

Maggie knew that was not true but nodded nonetheless.

"Doctor Suharto said I'll be here a couple more months; at least until my hallucinations and delusions stop," Chloe said. Her foot stopped bouncing and she turned to speak quietly to Maggie. "I think that alien that always stands behind Doctor Suharto is making him do things so that I go to prison. What do you think?"

Maggie did not know what to think. "I don't know how it goes."

"How about you?" Chloe asked, as her foot returned to bobbing. "You've been here the same length of time as me. What did the doctor tell you?"

Maggie was sad, she did not want to talk about it, but Chloe would pester her if she did not answer. "I guess I'm scheduled to go to trial."

"Oh, shit," Chloe said. "That's intense. I bet it's that black-robed guy I see following you around, he's probably telling Doctor Suharto to make your life miserable."

Maggie's jaw dropped. She had no idea Chloe could see that vampirish creature that comes to her at night to feed. "You can see it?"

"Of course I can see it," Chloe said, matter-of-factly. "I don't see it now, but I know it's around here someplace."

Maggie was not sure how to take what Chloe had said. Chloe was crazy; she saw aliens and believed they talked to the doctor. But she also saw the black-robed entity that both she and Ethel could see. Well, at least Ethel said she could see it; maybe she was lying. So either she, and Ethel, were as crazy as Chloe, or Chloe was not crazy at all and had the ability to see things others could not.

"Med time," one of the workers said from behind a table in the corner of the day room. "Ackerman."

"That's me," Chloe said, standing. "Time to get some more mind control meds."

Maybe I am crazy, Maggie thought as she watched Chloe walk to the med room where a nurse was dispensing medication. If I am crazy, the thing that feeds on me is not real. But the doctor said I was not crazy, and I don't think I'm crazy. I just cannot win. If I am not crazy, I have to stand trial and possibly go to prison for a crime that I did not commit. But if I am crazy, I'll have to stay locked up in a mental institution for the rest of my life.

Maggie began to sob. No one came to her aid as she sat there, alone, with tears streaming down her flushed face.

CONNIE MYRES

TWO

ETHEL DROVE INTO the parking lot of Port Glenn Psychiatric and Forensic Hospital. If it were not for the razor wire security fence around the perimeter, it would look like any modern hospital or office building. She took a final puff of the wood tip cigar she held in her arthritic hand before putting it out in the ashtray of her old gray sedan. She looked in the rearview mirror and adjusted the green polyester scarf tied around her head. She picked up her slouchy hobo handbag and got out of her old jalopy.

A cool breeze flapped her balloon sleeves and gypsy skirt as she walked to the main entrance. She could feel small pebbles through the souls of her moccasins as she walked along the long concrete sidewalk.

She walked inside the large three-story building and across the shiny-floored lobby to the front desk.

"I'm here to see Margaret McGee," Ethel said with her sandpapery voice.

The female guard shoved a paper in front of her. "Fill out this form, and I'll need a picture ID."

Ethel knew the drill; she had been visiting nearly every weekend since Maggie's admission to the high-security forensic center. She had her driver's license ready and a quarter for the lockers in which to lock her purse. When she was cleared to go in, she followed the guard through a metal detector and down a lengthy corridor to a locked section of the hospital. She followed the guard inside and into a visiting room where another guard sat at a desk. She filled out another form, chose a seat at the far end of the glassed partition, and waited for them to bring Maggie for her to see.

Several minutes had passed before Maggie walked in with one of the dayroom workers. Ethel waved so that Maggie would see her. Maggie walked over to Ethel and sat down in a plastic chair on the other side of the security glass. She picked up the phone.

"Hi Maggie," Ethel said, forcing a smile. It was difficult to smile while looking at Maggie's sad expression and drooping shoulders. "How are you doing?"

Maggie shrugged. "Fine, I suppose."

After talking about what Maggie ate for lunch, and her other daily activities such as sitting in the small library and staring at the wall, Ethel jumped into the more serious questions before her visiting time was up.

"When is your court date?" Ethel asked.

"It's September eleventh," Maggie said. "Have you made any progress . . . helping me?"

Ethel smiled and nodded as if things were going well, but she was actually making little progress. At her apartment, she could hear Debbie and Bruce on the second floor laughing in glee, something she had never heard until Maggie had moved in. At times, she sensed them coming down to the main floor and standing outside her apartment door. These so-called visits coincided with the times Ethel was casting spells of protection for Maggie and herself. But the spells were weak since they did not seem to bother Debbie and Bruce much because they would mock her before disappearing. "I'm going to call Detective Becker, again, and this time I'm going to talk to him in person; I might be able to get further with him."

Maggie did not say anything; instead, she looked down at the desktop.

"There's a new manager who comes out periodically and checks the place," Ethel said. "They want me to move out, but I don't want to. My lease isn't up and I want to stay close to the . . . others, because I have a stronger effect on them and I'm sure there's something we're missing when it comes to your defense."

"You still believe I didn't do it, don't you?" Maggie asked, looking up with moist eyes.

"Of course, dear, there's no doubt in my mind," Ethel said, reaching her bent arthritic fingers across the table. She would have held Maggie's hand if it were not for the partition. "I have an appointment to speak with your doctor while I'm here. He just wanted to talk over the phone, but I insisted I speak to him in person; it makes it easier to read him."

"Thanks, Ethel," Maggie said. She wiped her eye with a worn tissue. "Not knowing what will happen in court is killing me. It's like a heavy burden on me . . . like a weight made of darkness."

"How are you sleeping?" Ethel asked. Her eyes narrowed with concern.

"Not well," Maggie said, still holding the wet tissue. "I feel the dark robed entity feed on me, on my mental pain. You'd think that if he was feeding on my despair that it would be sucked out of me, but instead it seems like it is fueled." She touched the side of her neck. "I even feel bite marks in my neck, but I never see anything, I just feel these bumps under my skin."

Ethel looked at Maggie's neck and then down at her own arthritic hands, hands that she wished held a glass of bourbon whiskey . . . a tall glass of bourbon whiskey on the rocks. Then it occurred to her that maybe she should move because it has been over two months and she had made no progress with weakening Debbie and Bruce, and Susie for that matter. She felt she had no effect on the evil parasite attached to Maggie. She would need to take drastic measures. She looked back up at Maggie. "Don't worry; I have one more thing I can try."

"What's that?" Maggie asked.

"The crystal ball," Ethel said. Her hands trembled.

Maggie frowned. "That's too dangerous. You know what happened the last time the crystal ball was used; it brought that demon through and it hasn't left."

"It brought the demon through, it can send the demon back," Ethel said, forming a steeple with her knobby, red-nailed fingers.

"Even when the demon is here with me?" Maggie asked while still touching her neck.

"I may need Claudia to help me, especially since she was the one using it when the demon came through," Ethel said, trying hard to sound confident.

"But even if you and Claudia are able to make the demon, Debbie, Bruce, and Susie go away, it won't help me in court," Maggie said, dropping her hand to the tabletop. "It won't change the evidence."

Ethel sighed. "It might not change the evidence, but it will keep them from framing you any further and keep them from talking into the lawyers and other people's ears."

Maggie gave a halfhearted smile. "I suppose."

Ethel looked at her watch. "My time is almost up. Is there anything you need?"

Maggie shrugged, and then said, "Before you go, I need to know something."

"Sure, what's on your mind?" Ethel said, leaning toward the glass.

"You do see the spirits, don't you?" Maggie asked, looking Ethel straight in the eyes.

"I sense them, with my third eye," Ethel said, touching her forehead. She noticed Maggie look to the side in despair. "But don't you worry, I know they're there."

Maggie looked back at Ethel with tears in her eyes. "You don't think I'm crazy, do you?"

Ethel shook her head. "No, you're not crazy. Debbie and Bruce lured you to Sandpiper Bluff, back to the old psychiatric hospital where you worked in a previous life. Debbie and Bruce are selfish and evil spirits; they will do whatever they can to live here on Earth in their so-called existence of ecstasy. They will do whatever it takes to keep the dark entity happy . . . otherwise, their next stop is Hell. So, needless to say, they're highly motivated."

THREE

ETHEL WATCHED MAGGIE leave with a worker through a set of doors while she walked up to the guard's desk.

"I have an appointment with Doctor Suharto," Ethel said, smoothing the front of her colorful tiered skirt.

The guard looked confused, not to mention a little bewildered by Ethel's Boho-chic attire. "Doctor Suharto doesn't usually see people on weekends. Are you sure you have the right day?"

Ethel knew she had the right day. She had sent a spell his way, convincing him to make an exception for her. He did. "Could you please check it for me?"

The guard acted as if he was wasting his time when he picked up the phone. "This is Tony in the visiting area. Is Doctor Suharto expecting a visitor today?" There was a pause as the guard waited for an answer. "Oh. She's here, I'll send her over."

Ethel was relieved her spells were still strong . . . at least on normal people. She had not used them much before Maggie moved into the apartment building.

The guard made another phone call. "I have a visitor here who needs to be escorted to Doctor Suharto's office." He hung up and looked at Ethel.

Ethel smiled and tilted her head as she ran her fingers over her beaded neckless. "Is everything okay?"

The guard did not smile back. "Someone will be down in a minute to escort you to his office."

"Thank you."

Ethel turned and walked far enough away from the desk so that she would not block the path of other visitors. She looked back to where she and Maggie had sat. Her heart sank when she saw it empty, knowing Maggie was taken back into the belly of the giant beast of a building. She was mad at herself for not trying harder to help Maggie. The court date was only days away and she had not pressured the detective hard enough. She would make a point of it when she got back to her apartment.

Ethel tried not to listen in on conversations between the patients and the visitors while she waited for her escort, but it was difficult not to hear them. Talk of kids, court, and the weather was the talk of the day. One patient became

CONNIE MYRES

angry, accusing the hospital, the doctor, the lawyer, and whomever she could think of, for treating her badly. Was Maggie being treated badly? She did not think so; she did not get a sense of it when she was speaking with Maggie.

The door to the visitor room opened and a guard came in.

Wade pointed toward Ethel. "She needs to be escorted to Doctor Suharto's office."

"Follow me," the female guard said, looking momentarily surprised by the wrinkled woman's appearance.

"Thank you," Ethel said, following her out the door.

They walked further down the hall to an elevator where they both got inside. Neither one spoke as the elevator was pulled up to the third level. They stepped out and walked down the hall to an office marked with the doctor's name on a placard outside the door. They walked inside to a reception window. The guard stood back and motioned for Ethel to speak.

Ethel turned toward the receptionist. "I'm Ethel Dory. I have an appointment with Doctor Suharto." She could tell her rough voice was getting on the receptionist's nerves.

The young woman, with braided hair, looked down at the computer screen and then looked up at Ethel without raising her head. "Have a seat."

Ethel sat down in an office chair while the guard stood nearby. She was used to people giving her weird looks, as if she were a nomadic gypsy having just arrived in a covered wagon, looking to swindle whatever she could from the unsuspecting townsfolk. Nevertheless, she thought their behavior was unusual, especially for a hospital known to be tolerant of all people, no matter their race, color, or national origin. She was not even a full-blooded gypsy. When the Nazis had shot most of her ancestors on sight in the early 1940s, some managed to make their way to America; eventually abandoning their nomadic ways in the new country.

Then Ethel's heart skipped a beat. It could be possible that the spell she cast to speak with the doctor had side effects, had a sour side. That was not good. If her spells of good also had undesirable consequences, she was facing even more of an uphill battle to free Maggie.

It has to be the spirits, Ethel thought. They are strong, especially the black-robed one that feeds on Maggie. They apparently had the ability to counter her spells, making them bitter and acetous.

The door next to the receptionist window opened and the receptionist stood there, looking at Ethel. "Ms. Dory."

Ethel stood up and followed the receptionist, down a brightly lit hall, to the doctor's office, the guard trailing behind.

The receptionist walked up to the open office door. "Ethel Dory is here to see you."

"Please, come in," Dr. Suharto said with an Indonesian accent. He stayed seated as Ethel walked in and the guard and receptionist remained outside. "What can I do for you today, Ms. Dory?"

"I came to speak with you about Maggie McGee," Ethel said, nervously rubbing the dry skin on her forearm.

"Are you family?" the doctor asked, thumbing through papers.

"I'm a close friend," Ethel said. "I believe Maggie put me down as someone to whom you can share her personal information with. I'm also her emergency contact person."

"So, I see you are," he said. He looked up at her. "Margaret McGee is no longer considered IST, incompetent to stand trial, and has a court date of September eleventh scheduled."

Ethel was not sure how to approach the subject of ghosts and tell the doctor it was a spirit, of a child no less, that actually murdered Mr. Zimmerman. If she did, he would be committing her to the psych ward.

"Doctor Suharto," Ethel began, "Maggie is innocent; she was framed for the murder of Mr. Zimmerman."

"I see," the doctor said, not seeming to believe her.

"Do you believe in spirits, Doctor Suharto?" Ethel asked, as butterflies—or maybe wasps— flew around inside her queasy stomach.

"Are you talking about ghosts?" the doctor asked, closing the folder he had been looking at.

Ethel nodded timidly.

"There is no such thing as ghosts," he said.

"Do you believe in God?" Ethel asked. She watched as he pushed the folder to the side of his desk as if he had no interest in speaking about the topic.

"I am agnostic," he said, not making eye contact. "I neither believe nor disbelieve in God."

"Well, if you believe there could be a God, then you could believe there are angels," she said. "And if there are angels there are demons, Satan being one." Ethel wiped her sweaty palm on her skirt. "You are right, Maggie is sane. I don't know what she has told you, but I know she did not say she committed the crime." Ethel cleared the mucus that was building in her throat. "I'll get to the point. I am a seer and I know for a fact, Doctor, that there are spirits in this world, both good and bad. And I know that Maggie has been pursued by jealous spirits intent on causing her harm. I know this sounds way out, but there is even a dark-robed vampire spirit that feeds on her despair while she sleeps." She looked nervously at the doctor, waiting for him to tell her she was out of her mind and had to leave.

Dr. Suharto rubbed a brow. "Even if what you say is true, what does it have to do with me? My report states the facts based on my sessions with Ms. McGee." He sat down his pen and leaned back in his chair. "Have you seen one of these spirits?"

"I see them with my mind's eye," Ethel said, touching her temple. "But they are there and it is a fact. There are even studies that can prove it."

"What studies are you referring to?" the doctor asked, staring at her.

Ethel was not sure how to answer because she knew of no studies. "I can't think of any particular ones, but I'm sure you are aware of them."

"Ms. McGee suffers from hallucinations brought on by the stress of her husband's suicide, his infidelity with her best friend, and the stress of moving to a new home. She is now receiving the proper medicine and treatment to address this issue."

You fool, Ethel thought. "What motive would she possibly have for taking the superintendent's life?"

"There are no rational reasons in cases like these," he said.

"Well, I want it put on the record that Maggie is innocent and that it was spirits that killed Mr. Zimmerman," Ethel said, raising her chin like a child stubbornly refusing a wrongdoing.

"While it is true that Maggie has never said that she did not cause Mr. Zimmerman any harm, she has stated that spirits were the cause of his death. Hallucinations are real, as real as you and me, to the person suffering from them. They truly believe they see and hear things that are not there. I have no doubt she believes what she tells me, and you, but it is a symptom of schizophrenia, an inherited disease. She is now receiving proper medical and psychological care and is able to go to court and face the charges brought against her."

"But what about me?" Ethel said, crossing her arms. "Am I hallucinating and schizophrenic? How can both of us be affected by the same spirits?"

"I suggest that some of Ms. McGee's hallucinations could have been made worse by your talk of spirits to her and by you believing what she said, adding fuel to the fire."

Ethel was furious. Now the doctor was accusing her of making Maggie's mental illness worse. That is if she even had a mental illness. "How do you know she has schizophrenia? Is there a blood test?"

"No blood test," the doctor said, leaning back in his chair. "The diagnosis of schizophrenia is based on my observations during our interviews. While it appears she has not had symptoms for more than six months, she does report recent hallucinations, delusions, lack of energy, poor grooming habits, and a family history of schizophrenia."

"So are you saying that her symptoms did not begin until she moved to Sandpiper Bluff?" Ethel asked. "Surely that has to say something. The place used to be called Lake Shore Sanatorium and Psychiatric Hospital until it was later converted to apartments. The place is haunted." Ethel raised her voice. "That must mean something?"

The doctor turned his chair and looked out the window, watched a sparrow land on the windowsill, and then turned back to Ethel. "Ms. Dory, I have listened to your concerns and know you care about your friend. I suggest you study schizophrenia, psychosis, and hallucinations and educate yourself on mental illnesses," he stood up. "Maggie is mentally ill, she is not pursued by ghosts."

Ethel noticed her hands quivering more than usual. She wanted a smoke and a drink. She stood up and collected her composure. "Thank you, Doctor, for your time, but I suggest you do some reading on spirits, especially the evil ones." She walked out of the room.

The guard was not walking fast enough as she rushed down the corridor. Ethel wanted out of the building so that she could think about what she had to do next to help Maggie. She would call Det. Becker, even though she had no new evidence, but she could not just walk away from the case. She had the feeling the detective knew there was something else going on, but she did not know if the feeling was strong enough for him to act upon it.

They reached the last checkpoint and Ethel was free of the guard. She retrieved her purse from the locker and walked out of the building toward her car. Her hip began to ache from her exaggerated steps as she scrambled to the parking lot. She got into her car and took a wood tip cigar from her purse. She lit it, puffed, and then exhaled the smoke, allowing a little tension to flow out with it.

"I'm calling Claudia," she said, her voice cracked from the phlegm in her parched throat. "I don't want to use the crystal ball, but I don't see any other way to put an end to this madness."

The tires of the old gray sedan squealed as she rushed past rows of parked cars. "Hang in there Maggie, I'll help you."

FOUR

THE SUN WAS low on the western horizon when she drove past the realtor's For Sale sign and down the long, secluded driveway to Sandpiper Bluff Apartments. She slowed the car when the dilapidated three-story 1899 converted sanatorium came into view. Once magnificent and inviting, it now looked dark and ominous. No lights shined warmly in the windows; there was not even a working outdoor light to illuminate the front entrance. She was the only one now living in the building, which was beginning to look its age. She felt a sense of foreboding as if something bad was going to happen. Maybe not that night, but sometime soon. She felt uneasy because her feelings, her intuitions, were usually correct.

She pulled into the parking lot and turned off the car. She looked up at the third floor where the murdered superintendent, Mr. Carl Zimmerman, once lived. She felt sad for not checking on the beer-bellied, gray-haired man. She had thought he was just keeping to himself, which was typical of him. The new superintendent, Tim Chandler, was a young guy who refused to live in the building. He was hired by the owners, who now had the place up for sale.

She had received a letter from them telling her that she needed to make plans to move. She laughed when she read it. Only ghost hunters would want to buy a place where people were murdered and that was said to be haunted. Besides, she was not ready to move. She had an attachment to the place ever since she was a receptionist there back in the 1960s, back when it was called Lake Shore Sanatorium and Psychiatric Hospital. That was when the manager allowed her and Claudia Suttle to hold séances, but that was mostly because he liked the regular contact with his deceased wife.

However, it was not long before he became a drunkard and the psychiatric hospital was mismanaged. Especially when it became known that the staff was mistreating the patients. The final nail in the coffin was when a ten-year-old mentally ill child was admitted with an antisocial personality disorder. One moment she was calm and sweet, and the next she became violent. She was so unpredictable that she gained access to bandage scissors and killed an orderly in 1969. The place closed shortly thereafter.

The séances ended as well. Actually, Ethel put an end to the séances earlier in 1969, before the place was closed. It was Claudia's turn to be the medium during a séance. She was in the basement scrying room using the crystal ball, just like they always did to speak with spirits. Assisting clients who wanted to talk with deceased loved ones so that they would know they were well and not to worry. However, when a grieving couple wanted to communicate with their young daughter who had died from influenza; that was when the dark entity entered the room instead of the child. She and Claudia were unable to banish the strong entity as it stayed in the building feeding off patients and staff. Soon weak souled people and staff with a penchant for wrongdoing—like the nurse Debbie Franklin and Doctor Bruce Hancock— became violent and uncaring toward patients. They were easy targets for the entity, allowing it to use them in exchange for eternal ecstasy. But the entity wanted a pure soul in exchange for the eternal sexual rapture between the two lowlifes. It wanted a nurse named Margaret.

Enough thinking of that, Ethel said to herself. She did not want to go inside where the spirits Debbie and Bruce roamed the second floor in their promised bliss, but her apartment was safe. Ethel's spells were strong enough to keep the spirits from harming her, but the longer Maggie stayed in despair, the stronger the black-robed spirit became. And it granted some of the strength he acquired to Debbie and Bruce. Ethel knew would soon need to move whether or not the manager wanted her out of the building.

Ethel envisioned a white light around her body as she got out of the car. She would need to go down in the basement of the building, to the scrying room, to get the crystal ball that had been locked up there since 1969. But she would not do that alone. She would call Claudia and have her come over and go with her to the basement to retrieve it.

She slung the hobo bag over her shoulder and limped to the porch. Her hip ached from the long car ride and the previous fall in Maggie's apartment.

The once full and frilly ferns, hanging above the porch rails, were dead. The porch swing that once swayed gently in the Lake Michigan breeze was covered with white and gray bird droppings. Even the once pleasant scent of roses and spruce trees had changed to rotting wood and a decaying animal underneath the floorboards.

She walked into the vestibule, unlocked the glass panel door to the lobby, and went inside. She focused on keeping herself protected as she walked swiftly past the superintendent's office to her first-floor apartment. Once inside, she locked her door and breathed a sigh of relief. She turned around and was about to take the bag from her shoulder when she saw writing on the living room window. She walked cautiously up to the window facing the lake. The writing was on the outside of the pain of glass and appeared to have been written in red lipstick. It said: WATCHING YOU.

Ethel immediately dropped her purse and moved quickly to the gold tin box on a bookshelf. She opened it, took the canister of blessed salt, and began reapplying it at the base of the door and windows. She wanted to apply it around all the perimeter walls, but she did not have enough. Then she took out a sage smudging stick and a turkey feather. She lit the bundle of herbs with a match from a box sitting next to a pack of wood-tip cigars on the side table by the couch and began smudging the apartment. Fanning the smoke with the feather as she moved room to room, corner to corner. When she smudged by the message on the window, it began dripping like blood, down the windowpane. She closed the curtain and continued the cleansing.

When she was done, she put the items back into the box and placed it respectfully back into its place on the shelf. Then she lit a thin cigar before picking up the telephone and calling Claudia.

"Hello," said a loud, whiny voice.

"Claudia, I need a favor," Ethel said, speaking swiftly.

"What favor?" Claudia asked with a sharp tone.

"You remember Maggie McGee, don't you?" Ethel said, knowing Claudia was not happy. She took a drag of the cigar.

"Sure," Claudia said. "She's the sweet girl who seems to attract bad things to her."

"Well, she needs my help, and I need your help," Ethel said. She could hear Claudia open what sounded like the refrigerator and crack the tab of a can, probably beer, she thought.

"I know what you're going to say and I'm against it," Claudia said. Her high-pitched voice reverberated through the phone line.

"I can't do the séance by myself," Ethel said. "I need your help and I need the . . . crystal ball."

Claudia choked and hacked. "No way, Ethel. The demon that came through it years ago almost killed me. I already cannot see worth a damn because of it. The crystal ball needs to stay locked up. Why do you think we need to use it again?"

Ethel had thought about the answer in advance, knowing Claudia would be a hard sell. "Because the demon is attached to Maggie and feeding off her, not to mention the two evil spirits, Debbie and Bruce, are doing everything they can to sabotage any help sent her way. The crystal ball is powerful and is the only way we can send the demon back to where it came from . . . Hell."

The sound of the phone being slammed against something and then picked up, rang through Ethel's ear.

"Or, Ethel, it could bring another demon through the gateway to Hell. If that were to happen, you are not strong enough to fight off two of them. They would reach into our bodies and take our souls back through the gateway with them. Are you willing to take that chance?" Claudia said.

Ethel sighed. "Together we are two strong mediums, and I think we have a chance against the demon and the evil spirits. If we do not try, Maggie will live the rest of her life in agony, in a living Hell on Earth. Besides, we're a couple old hags, what do we have to lose?"

"You know what we have to lose," Claudia said, "our souls."

"But I have something that will give us the edge," Ethel said.

"What?" Claudia said.

"I don't have it yet," Ethel said. "But when Debbie, Bruce, and sadly Margaret, were blown to pieces in that boating accident out on Lake Michigan in 1969, their personal belongings were left in their lockers. I don't think anyone ever removed them because the hospital was shut down shortly after that. I can use their personal items to conjure up a spell to send them to Hell."

"I'm not liking your idea, Ethel," Claudia said.

"It's worth trying to find things they possessed," Ethel said. "The staff locker room for the nurses was in the basement. I think the doctors kept their things in the doctors' lounge on the third floor. I think that all we need is one thing from any one of them."

"Are you saying that when the building was renovated no one ever opened or removed the lockers?" Claudia said.

"I don't think so," Ethel said. "When I was down in the locker room, years ago now, they appeared to be walled over and the room was used for storage. I think we can hammer our way through the drywall and get to them."

"If that were the case," Claudia said. "How would we know which lockers were theirs?"

"Because, as you know, I was the receptionist during that time and I had access to the list of who had which locker," Ethel said.

"How are you going to find a decade's old paper?" Claudia said.

"The file cabinet is in the storage room," Ethel said. "When the place closed, a lot of the paperwork was just left behind."

"Like I said, what if we can't find the paper you're after?" Claudia asked.

"I know all the staff took their things out of the lockers when they left. So the lockers with personal items left behind would be Debbie's, Bruce's, and Margaret's." Ethel said. She paused and then said, "Wait a minute, you said we. Are you with me then?"

"It was a slip of the tongue," Claudia said. "Why would I be in on something that is such a long shot and likely to send us to the inferno?"

"Because you and I are good people and care about setting the wrongs to right," Ethel said. "Maggie needs our help and we are the only ones who can help her. And you know as well as I do that the actions we take in this life will decide the fate of our future existences . . . karma. I do not want my destiny to be that of a slug. And even if the demon is able to take us back to Hell with him, we will not go unrewarded for our good deed. What goes around comes around."

The phone slammed against something again. "Damn it, Ethel, I'm pissed off."

"I can tell," Ethel said, smiling. She knew Claudia was being convinced to help.

"Okay, I'll do it," Claudia said. "So when is all this going to happen?"

"Stop over tomorrow afternoon," Ethel said.

FIVE

"JOHNNY, I THOUGHT I was the only one crazy enough to work late on a Saturday," Det. Haley Wanat said walking to her desk with a folder in hand. "Is it the McGee case?"

Det. John Becker looked up from the computer screen. He and Det. Wanat was the only ones in the office of the homicide division on the second floor in the Black Water Police Department that Saturday evening. "Yeah, I keep thinking there's something I'm missing."

"I think you're overly attached to that case," Detective Wanat said, sitting at her desk across from his. "You should go home and get some sleep."

Det. Becker stood and went to the coffee machine. He poured himself a cup of black coffee and walked back to his desk. "The preliminary testing showed Ms. McGee's DNA

CONNIE MYRES

on the knife, along with Carl Zimmerman's, but there were also a few other sets of DNA."

"Are you thinking that the suspect's DNA was incidental from the dirty clothes in the laundry basket where it was found?" she asked, watching Det. Becker sip the coffee, make a face, and then sit down.

"It's a possibility," he said. "But the other DNA was degraded; it appeared to be old DNA. It's going to take forensics longer to profile it."

"Have you determined where the weapon was purchased?" she asked.

"Purchased?" The detective snickered. "This karambit dates back to the twelfth century, probably Indonesia. It appears to be more a museum piece rather than something purchased from a munitions store. I find it hard to believe the suspect has an interest in this type of weaponry when nothing in her apartment, house, or history shows that. Also, I have found no place that sells karambits of that age. Even Mr. Zimmerman has no history of purchasing weapons of that type."

"Was it stolen?" she asked, flipping open a folder.

"There are no reports of stolen or missing weapons of that type," he said, and then sipped the hot, burnt coffee and sat it on his desk, away from the computer and paperwork.

"So it was passed down in a family?" she asked.

"Possibly," he said, looking at the computer screen. "But none of the suspect's family or friends ever reports seeing a weapon of that type."

"What about that fortune teller?" she asked, tapping her pen on the desktop.

"Ethel Dory," he said, letting out a sigh. "She's quite the character. I am going to speak with her again. She adamantly defends the suspect, even to the point that she states evil spirits framed Ms. McGee."

"You can't take a ghost to trial." She laughed.

"No shit." He rubbed the back of his aching neck and watched Det. Wanat give him an amused look.

"The best you can do is clear Ms. McGee of the crime, and leave the case open," she said. "If she is innocent. Or she could just be crazy; she was sent to the psych hospital, after all."

He nodded and reached for the white Styrofoam cup. He was about to take another sip but decided the brown liquid inside was deadly, just like the killer who slashed the superintendent.

SIX

ETHEL WAS LOOKING through her book of spells early that Sunday afternoon when the buzzer sounded. She got up and walked to the wall panel.

"Yes?" she said.

"This is Detective Becker, homicide detective from the Black Water Police Department; is this Ethel Dory?" he asked.

"Yes, Detective, please come in," Ethel said, buzzing him in. She quickly put the book of spells back on the bookshelf and walked to the front door. She had been casting subtle white spells his way, beckoning him to open his eyes and search for the truth behind Mr. Zimmerman's murder. She wanted to tell him she was expecting him as she opened the door and the detective approached, but decided against it. "Come in, please, Detective."

"Thank you," he said, walking into her cozy Victorian-style apartment. "What is that smell? Marijuana?"

She closed the door. "Heavens no, it's sage. I use it for protection. Please sit down." She pointed toward the sofa.

He looked at the old lumpy flowered cushions and opted to stand. He took a small notepad and pen from the inside breast pocket of his suit coat. "I apologize for stopping by unexpectedly, but I had a few more questions about Margaret McGee."

Ethel sat on the couch. "Not a problem, Detective." She took a wood tip cigar and was about to light it, and then stopped. "Do you mind?"

He shook his head and watched her spark the thin brown cylinder of tobacco leaves. "I have a few questions about the karambit."

"Karambit?" Ethel asked, squishing her eyebrows together.

"The knife found in Ms. McGee's apartment," he said. He took a photograph from his breast pocket. "Here is a picture of it. Have you seen it before?"

"I believe you've asked about the knife already," Ethel said, taking the picture. She looked at the curved crescent blade, stained with what she assumed was Mr. Zimmerman's blood. It made her think of a cat's claw or a hook, a few inches long. "No, I've never seen a knife like this before. It's a rather odd knife, where is it from?"

"Knives of this type are from Southeast Asia," he said. "This particular one appears to be from Indonesia and dates back to the twelfth century. It probably was used to rake roots and to plant rice in fields. Later, it was found to make a good weapon because its curved blade maximized its cutting potential. It was a popular weapon of women who would tie it into their hair and use it in self-defense."

"You're kidding," Ethel said, handing back the photograph. "I can tell you, I've never seen Maggie with it, or any weapon. She has never even talked about weapons."

Ethel chanted a spell for the truth to be revealed, silently in her mind. With Detective Becker so close to her, it was bound to be effective.

Detective Becker looked around the room and decided to sit in a chair at Ethel's small round table; the one where she typically cast spells. "I thought about what you said and did more research on this building."

Ethel smiled. "Yes, please continue."

"I found that you were a receptionist here when it was known as Lake Shore Sanatorium and Psychiatric Hospital and that there was a murder here shortly before it closed down."

Ethel nodded. "Yes, that was terrible. I remember it well."

"Would you mind telling me what you remember?" he asked.

Ethel puffed her cigar. "I was the receptionist on duty when they brought in the young girl;

she was around ten years old, I believe. Anyway, the nurses always talked with me, when they were going off shift. Confidentiality was not as big of thing back then, in 1969. They told me about how unpredictable the young girl was, how she would be so sweet and obedient one moment, and then without warning would turn into someone possessed. I believe her name was Susie Knight. I don't know the young girl's family history. Anyway, I remember the day of the murder being chaotic. Patients were extra violent and the nurses were on edge, ready to quit and walk out the door." She puffed the cigar. "The doctor on duty that day was Doctor Bruce Hancock. He was typically nonchalant, but that day he seemed on edge. I don't know if it was because he was mentoring a young doctor who was working on becoming a psychiatrist, or just because it was one of those days."

"Do you remember the young doctor's name?" he asked.

"No, but he was from another country and spoke with broken English," she said. She thought a moment and then said, "There are old documents in the basement that they never took when the place closed. Maybe his name is in there."

He looked up from the pad. "Yes, I would like to see them. I'll contact the owners and get permission to go through them."

Ethel nodded in agreement, but she and Claudia were going to go through them with or without permission when they searched for

Debbie and Bruce's lockers. She tapped the cigar ashes into a glass ashtray. "Soon there were screams, blood-curdling screams. And shouts to call the police and an ambulance as people ran down the stairs, tripping over each other. It was like a stampede of cattle rushing out of the building."

"What exactly happened with the girl and the victim?" he asked.

"The orderly had taken lunch in for the girl," Ethel said. "The nurses were busy, and Susie was looking sad and I guess he must have felt sorry for her, so he decided to unrestrain her so that she could feed herself. Then a nurse went into the room and I guess she had a pair of bandage scissors in her pocket. Somehow, the girl was able to grab them and she began stabbing the orderly who was helping her do something and she ended up . . . killing the young man, Damian Richards. It makes me sad to think about it."

"Do you know what happened to the scissors?" Det. Becker asked.

"No, I never saw the scissors," Ethel said. "Come to think of it, no one ever talked about the scissors. I think I learned about them in a news story in the local paper. But that's not the end of the little girl's problems. After the murder she was apparently kept restrained continuously and then she was accidentally killed by suffocation, I guess, because of one of the nurses' negligence."

"Is there anything else you remember about that time?" he asked.

"Not really," she said. "We were told not to talk about it, except when answering the investigators questions. And that is how it was until two more deaths occurred."

"Two more deaths?" he said, resting an elbow on the table so that he could quickly take notes. "Tell me about them."

Ethel now had her chance to talk about Debbie and Bruce. Hopefully, he would see how they fit into the picture. "It didn't happen here at the hospital but out on a boat on Lake Michigan, not far from this place. Two nurses, I think their names were Deborah and Margaret, along with Doctor Hancock, and the boat's captain were all killed. I guess the boat blew up from a gas leak." She leaned forward. "Detective, I know you don't believe in spirits and that these things happened a long time ago, but could you please humor me and do some research on the nurses, the doctor, the little girl, and the weapon? I just have the feeling you might find the answers you seek."

Det. Becker did not say anything as he put the notepad and pen back into his pocket. "I will be back to go through the documents in the basement." He stood up and looked around the room. Wallpaper with elaborate floral designs was on two walls, while red curtains, embroidered with poppies, hung from a brass rod over the front window. "Have you found another place to live?"

Ethel stood up, reaching the door before Detective Becker. "Not yet." She paused, and then said, "There is one more thing you need to know before you go."

He stopped at the door and looked at her. "What is that?"

"Back in 1969 my friend Claudia and I were conducting séances in the basement—all legit mind you and with the manager's permission— but we inadvertently conjured up an evil spirit, a demon. After that had happened, things went from bad to worse here at the hospital. Staff began abusing patients and the little girl, Susie, murdered the orderly not long afterward." She studied his reaction. She was relieved when he did not laugh or dismiss her remarks. Good, maybe there was a little bit of him that was beginning to believe her story. "That demon and the evil spirits are preying and feeding on Maggie. You have to help her, Detective."

Detective Becker stared at her and then said, "I'll do what I can."

Ethel was pleasantly surprised by his answer. She opened the door and stepped aside. "I'm glad you stopped by, Detective."

The detective walked out the door. Ethel watched him as he walked through the lobby. "We're counting on you, Detective."

SEVEN

ETHEL WAITED IN her car at the end of Sandpiper Bluff's long driveway. Claudia would be getting off the bus soon and she would give her a ride through the forest to the apartment building. The old sanatorium sat over half a mile away from the road on the edge of a bluff. It was typically refreshing, but this day, the day she and Claudia were planning to go down into the basement and look for items left in Debbie and Margaret's lockers decades ago, and then retrieve the crystal ball, was different. The air was thick and muggy, making breathing difficult. Ethel felt that the spirits, Debbie and Bruce, knew what they were up to and were preparing for it. Preparing to stop them.

The bus rumbled down the dirt road, stopping in front of the driveway. Ethel got out of the car to assist Claudia down the bus stairwell. Ever since the incident in 1969, when the demon came through the crystal ball and momentarily possessed Claudia—before taking up residency in the hospital—Claudia was left nearly blind, forcing her to wear thick cataract glasses and use a white cane.

"I'm fine, I'm fine," Claudia said, her voice loud and whiny as she resisted Ethel's help. "I'm not blind, you know."

"Good to see you again, Claudia," Ethel said, grinning. "Good to know you haven't changed; you're as cranky as ever."

"Good to see you too, you old bat," Claudia said, walking toward Ethel's clunker. "I can't believe you talked me into this."

Ethel lifted her below-the-knee gypsy skirt and climbed into the driver's seat of the suffocating car. She turned the ignition. Hot air from the vents blew into their faces.

Claudia lifted her edematous legs inside the car and then closed the door. She took off her shawl and sat it on the seat between her and Ethel. "You don't have air conditioning?" she grumbled.

Ethel looked over at Claudia's swollen lower extremities and beige compression stockings that stretched underneath her mid-calf Capri pants. "We don't have far to go."

Claudia shook her head. "I know how far we have to go. I've been here before, you know."

Ethel put the sedan in gear and drove slowly down the driveway. The pine and oak trees cast dark shadows along the narrow path;

the shade did not come close to making up for a failing air conditioner.

When they rounded the last curve in the driveway, the old sanatorium came into view. Claudia wiped perspiration from her brow as they left the shaded tunnel of trees and drove into the afternoon sun-soaked parking lot. They sat in the car looking at the old building and its once grand wraparound double-deck porches.

"I've got a bad feeling about this," Claudia said, squirming in her seat.

"All we have to do is find the lockers and get one of Debbie or Margaret's personal items." Ethel cleared her throat. "And we have to get the crystal ball."

Claudia twisted her cane into the car's dirty carpet. "Let's just get this over with."

Ethel and Claudia got out of the car. Claudia began wheezing as she plodded toward the sidewalk.

"Are you okay?" Ethel asked, walking up next to her.

"I'm fine," Claudia said, waddling along. "Let's just get somewhere cool. You do have air conditioning in your apartment, don't you?" She stopped and looked at Ethel.

Ethel avoided Claudia's glare. "Well, no. But I don't need it; I get the cool breeze that blows in from the lake."

Claudia looked at the surrounding trees. Not even an oak leaf was twitching or a pine branch swaying. "Nothing is blowing off Lake Michigan right now. There is no moving air.

The only breeze is from the flapping wings of those old crows flying away from this dump."

"Those aren't crows," Ethel said. Her voice faltered. "I think those big black birds are ravens. You don't usually find ravens in this part of Michigan."

Indeed, the air felt wet and heavy, like an overbearing fog. And the black ravens, yes, they had been growing in number ever since Maggie was sent away; growing into a murder of crows. It was as though they were claiming the building as their own or waiting as observers. Observers, patiently waiting for death to arrive. "The spirits know we're trying to stop them," Ethel said as she walked ahead of Claudia.

While Ethel opened the front door, Claudia took each step of the porch one at a time. Her waterlogged ankles kept her from moving as quickly as she wanted to. Not that she wanted to go inside the building with its evil spirits, but she needed to get out of the sun that was baking down upon them. It was not hot like this when she got on the bus in Black Water. There, the sun was shining, sure enough, but it was not suffocating, not unbearable.

Ethel held the door open as she watched Claudia finally reach the top step. She wanted to ask, once again, if Claudia needed help, but she was afraid that Claudia would whack her with her cane. "Do you need to set down on the porch swing?"

Claudia looked over at the swing covered in bird feces as the last of the glossy black avifauna flew away, joining the rest of the scattered ravens, who seemed to be watching them. She looked back at Ethel in disgust. "I don't think so."

The deep raspy call of the jet-black birds made the hair stand up on the nape of Ethel's neck. She knew that the ravens overtaking Sandpiper Bluff Apartments were likely a bad omen. They were harbingers of death and stealer of souls and they were surrounding the old hospital, like spectators in an ancient Roman arena waiting to watch those condemned to death be ripped apart by wild lions. "Hurry it up; I want to get to my apartment."

"Don't get your knickers in a knot," Claudia said, walking behind Ethel into the vestibule. "I'm going as fast as I can."

"At the speed you move, I'll be singing auld lang syne and bidding farewell to this year," Ethel said. She unlocked the lobby door and stepped into the dimly lit space.

"The way this year is turning out," Claudia said, following Ethel into the lobby, "that sounds like a good idea."

Ethel shivered as she stood in front of her apartment door, having outpaced Claudia across the reception area. "It's colder than usual in here."

As Claudia passed Mr. Zimmerman's old office, she stopped and looked over at the open stairway and its dingy banister leading to the second floor, and down to the basement. "I sense spirits here." She turned and walked up to Ethel. The plastered walls were cracked in such a manner that it looked like rusty veins were ripping through the interior. "This place is falling apart. I thought the owners were keeping this place up."

Ethel opened her apartment door and motioned for Claudia to follow her. "It was kept up, at least until Maggie moved in and the spirits grew stronger. Mr. Zimmerman kept the banister and floor polished to a glossy perfection. Things were shiny and clean." Ethel closed and locked the door as Claudia made her way to the couch. "And that was even between his drinking binges. But sad to say, the building's history and the reincarnated spirits have affected the structure."

Claudia used her cane to push aside a book, before putting her legs on the coffee table. "You need to get out of this place before something bad happens."

Ethel walked over to the bookshelf where she kept the gold tin box containing many of the items she needed to cast spells. She took it down and sat it on the small round table. "Let's get started with the prayer for protection."

"I just got comfortable," Claudia said, taking her legs off the coffee table. She grunted as she stood and walked to sit across from Ethel at the table.

Ethel lit the blessed white candle she had sitting in the center of the tabletop. Then she sat a picture of St. Patrick next to it and they said aloud:

The cross of Christ be with me;

The cross of Christ overcomes all water and every fire;

The cross of Christ overcomes all weapons;

The cross of Christ is a perfect sign and blessing to my soul.

May Christ be with me and my body during all my life

At day and at night. Now I pray, I pray God the Father

For the soul's sake, and I pray God the Son for the Father's sake,

And I pray God the Holy Ghost for the Father's and Son's sake,

And I pray God the Holy Ghost for the for the Father's and the Son's sake, . . .

As she said the prayer, the windowpanes began to vibrate, as if a giant bulldozer was driving up to the building, ready to demolish it. Ethel kept focused on the prayer. She took Claudia's hands and held them firmly as the afternoon sun, seeping in around the sides of the closed curtains, disappeared. Leaving the room dark.

That the holy corpse of God may bless me against all evil things, words and works.

The Cross of Christ

The cross of Christ open unto me future bliss;

The cross of Christ be with me, above me, before me,

Behind me, beneath me, aside of me and

Everywhere, and before all my enemies,

Visible and invisible; these all flee from me

As soon as they but know or hear.

Enoch and Elias, the two prophets, were never

Imprisoned, nor bound, nor beaten and came

Never out of their power; thus no one of my enemies

Must be able to injure or attack me in my body

Or my life, in the name of God the Father, the Son,

And the Holy Ghost. Amen!

Protection from Heaven

The blessing which came from heaven,

*From God the Father, when the true living
Son was born,*

Be with me at all times;

*The blessing which God spoke over the whole
human race,*

Be with me always.

Ethel finished the prayer, opened her eyes, and released Claudia's hands. The only light in the room was from the flickering candle. "It got dark outside."

Claudia watched Ethel stand and walk to the front window. "You did a good job protecting your apartment, but we still have to leave it and go down to that damned basement."

Ethel nodded and moved the curtain enough to peer outside. "It's dark outside. It's like there is a thick black fog surrounding the building."

"That demon is powerful," Claudia said. She stood and walked next to Ethel. "I hate to say it, but now we have to finish what we've started because they'll never leave us alone, if we don't. I'll be followed back to my house. It's not haunted now, but it soon will be."

"Oh my god," Ethel said. Her chin began to tremble.

"What?" Claudia said, stamping her cane on the floor like a child having a temper tantrum.

Ethel moved the curtain so that she could see the writing on the outside glass. Written in

CONNIE MYRES

what appeared to be fresh dripping blood were the words: WE ARE WAITING.

EIGHT

THEN A LOUD thump vibrated through the ceiling. Both Ethel and Claudia jumped.

"That came from Maggie's apartment," Ethel said, looking up at the ceiling. "They are definitely angry with us."

"I'm mad, too," Claudia said, walking to the kitchen.

"What are you doing?" Ethel said, closing the curtain.

Claudia opened and closed cabinet doors until she found what she was looking for, a bottle of bourbon whiskey. She poured a shot into a glass and drank it down as if it were a magic potion. "Want some?"

"Yeah, I do want some," Ethel said. "But we need to keep our wits about us while we do this. I don't wish to make any mistakes."

"The mistake is already done. I'm here helping you with this." She began opening drawers. "Where is your flashlight?"

Ethel walked into the spare room filled with Maggie's belongings. She pushed aside Maggie's suitcase and took a flashlight and a candlestick from a dresser drawer. Then she took the candle from the center of the table and placed it in the candlestick's cup. She turned to Claudia and handed her the flashlight. There was no way her wobbly body could safely handle a candle. "I appreciate your help; I couldn't do this without you."

Claudia walked to the door, raised her cane, and shouted a battle cry. "It's time to send the demon and its accomplices back to Hell."

"I'm glad you're all in," Ethel said, smiling as she walked to the door.

"I'm under the influence of false courage," Claudia said, returning to her unsteady gait. "We'd better hurry and get this done before I change my mind."

Ethel turned the deadbolt and then rested her hand on the doorknob. She looked at Claudia's tired, wrinkled face. She felt sorry for talking Claudia into helping her cast out the spirits, but she knew she was not strong enough to do it herself. She hoped her spell of protection was strong enough to protect them while they searched for what they needed. But when she looked at Claudia's thick cataract glasses, and fluid bloated body, supported by one wooden cane, she knew that simply falling down a staircase would be enough to likely kill Claudia or at least cripple her more than she already was. Nevertheless, she turned the knob and opened the door.

Icy air rushed into their faces, both refreshing and frightening at the same time.

Claudia sighed and followed Ethel out the door.

Ethel took the apartment key from her skirt pocket and locked the door behind them. They stood there a moment, watching shadows dance on the walls and ceiling. Some shadows were obviously cast from the candle's flames, but others seemed to move against the grain, or not move at all.

"I hope your ghosts didn't recruit help," Claudia said, shining her flashlight toward the lobby. "And why don't the lights work around here?"

Ethel held the candle and walked ahead, leading Claudia past Mr. Zimmerman's office and toward the stairway. "They used to, but this place has been having electrical problems."

Claudia shined her light toward the steps leading to the basement and then at the elevator and its open door. "Do you think it's safe to take the elevator?"

"Not really," Ethel said, looking at the black box. "But considering your condition I think we should use it."

"What do you mean, my condition?" Claudia said, shining the flashlight into Ethel's eyes.

"Okay, then, we'll take the stairs. Let's go," Ethel said walking to the lip of the open staircase, leading down into the basement. "Why do you have to be so contrary?"

Claudia ignored Ethel's remark and followed her, briefly shining the flashlight up the staircase to the second floor. Sounds of shuffling and a giggle echoed down through the darkness. "They're upstairs right now, but I'm sure they'll be following us."

"No doubt," Ethel said, taking one cautious step at a time.

When they reached the bottom step, the air was damp. An odor of mold and a rotting animal filled the air.

Claudia paused and shined the flashlight down the long hallway. "It's been decades since I've been down here. I remember the scrying room being down that way, and the kitchen being to the right, but I don't remember where the locker room was."

Ethel walked slowly to the room that was once the kitchen. "It's storage now."

Claudia followed Ethel. "Do you remember—before that demon from Hell came through—how we made people happy? They absolutely loved us. We were at the peak of our game. And the parties we would attend at the beach; they were the best."

"Of course I remember," Ethel said, stopping in front of the old kitchen. "If that demon never came into this place, it could have been turned into a lakeshore resort, rather than a building infested with spirits."

Claudia nodded and then shined her light through the open door. Remnants of counters, sinks, and stoves sat in the shadows behind old stretchers, beds, and wheelchairs.

Ethel brushed a cobweb from the door and walked into the room.

"What are you doing?" Claudia said. "The lockers aren't in there, are they?"

"No, but I might need a hammer or something to break through the wall," Ethel said, moving the candlestick side-to-side.

"First, let's see if we even need a hammer," Claudia said, shining her light back down the corridor. "Maybe they're not even behind a wall."

"I suppose," Ethel said, walking out. She walked to the next room. She tried to open the door, but it would not open. "It's locked."

"What room is that?" Claudia asked.

"I think this was where they kept medical records," Ethel said, turning away from the door. "But I know I saw file cabinets in the old locker room when I was down here a while back."

Claudia shined the light toward the next door along the wide hallway. The light reflected off a dusty old placard with words: EMPLOYEE LOCKER ROOM. "There it is."

Ethel opened the door. "Shine your light around for something to prop open this door."

Claudia shined the light around the room. Indeed, file cabinets stood along the side wall, next to an old desk. "How do you know the locker assignment list is in the file cabinet?"

"Because they're the file cabinets that were in the reception area when I worked here. At least I think so because I remember they were a gray metal and the height looks right," Ethel said. Then she walked up to a box filled with old hardcover medical books. She sat the candle on the desk and tried to push the box in front of the door. "Shine your light here so I can see."

Claudia lit the box of reference books: Gray's Anatomy of the Human Body and Taber's Cyclopedic Medical Dictionary added weight to the damp cardboard box. She watched as Ethel grunted and strained as she slid the heavy box in front of the door. "You're in pretty good shape for an old bitty."

Ethel moaned as she stood upright and placed a hand on her sore hip. "If you say so."

Claudia shined the light around the old plaster walls. "Why would they wall up the lockers?"

"They used this room as an office for a while when they first renovated it into apartments," Ethel said as she walked to the back wall. "Until the manager decided he didn't like being down here and moved the office to where it is now, on the first floor."

Claudia took her cane and begin rapping on the water-stained drywall of the back wall.

"Sounds hollow. There must be a space behind it."

"We need a way to break through it," Ethel said, rubbing her hip.

"Maybe you can saw through the sheetrock," Claudia said. "Where did Mr. Zimmerman keep his tools?"

"Outside in the shed," Ethel said, picking up the candlestick. "If we don't find anything down here, I'll have to go get a sledgehammer or something."

"I think you may have to," Claudia said, shining her light at fluttering cobwebs hanging from the ceiling. "I haven't seen anything, so far, that we can use to break through the wall."

"I don't want to leave you here by yourself," Ethel said. Then she jumped when she saw a mouse jump out of the box she had just moved and then scurry into a dark corner behind more boxes.

"I'll be fine," Claudia said, trying to open the top file cabinet drawer. After a few wiggles, the drawer opened. "I'll hunt for the locker list while you're gone. Where'd you keep it?"

Ethel walked up to the open drawer. She took a faded musty form from a folder. "This brings back memories; it's a daily visitor log. We definitely have the right cabinet. It's been decades since I've looked at this stuff, but I think we're on the right track."

"Here." Claudia said, handing Ethel the flashlight. "This will help you better than that candle when you go outside to the shed."

Ethel sat the candle on the desk and took the flashlight. "I'll be as fast as I can."

"I hope so," Claudia said, closing the top cabinet drawer.

Ethel walked out of the room. Claudia could hear her climb the stairs as she opened the next drawer. She picked up the candle so that she could read the folder tabs better. "I might have you," she said, setting the candle back onto the desk.

She took out the folder and laid it next to the candle so that she could read it better. She leaned her cane against the desk and began looking through the papers inside the folder. Then she heard footsteps coming back down the stairs.

"That was fast," Claudia said, her whiney voice echoing through the basement. Then she heard a second set of steps descending. Then a frigid gust of air caused her breath to show, just before the candle blew out.

NINE

ETHEL WALKED THROUGH the front door and onto the porch. It was dark. No moon, no stars, not even a light in the building. Even the beam of the flashlight seemed dim as it tried to penetrate the blackness.

She did not want to walk off the porch and into the air absent of light. But having no other good choices—other than getting into the car and driving away—she shined the muted shaft of light down to light her path. Then she heard the sound of something moving in the darkness not far from her. She stopped and listened, but the sound would stop as well. She was afraid to shine the light toward whatever seemed to be following her; she was afraid of what she might see.

She began walking again, and so did the thing following her, watching her. She stopped again and so did the footsteps. It was too quiet, not even the lapping waves of Lake Michigan seemed to be able to penetrate the thick air.

When Ethel reached the shed, she slid open the shed door, it screeched as it rolled along rusty runners. Before she walked inside, she looked past the bluff, toward the horizon, only the slightest of sunlight penetrated through the inky fog enveloping the property. The air felt heavy, as dark, undulating waves moved through the still, dark air.

She turned her attention back to the shed. She shined the light inside and saw several gardening tools, a shovel, and rake. Deeper in the shed she saw a toolbox and a limb saw, rope, a wheelbarrow, and an old snow blower.

"Come on, Mr. Zimmerman, you have to have a hammer around here someplace," she said, walking further inside. She did not want to go too far inside, fearing someone may come up behind her, slide the door shut and lock her inside.

Something scurried across the dirty concrete floor, as Ethel shined the light from corner to corner. Then she saw a sledgehammer and an ax. She went to pick up the large, heavy hammer that Mr. Zimmerman used to drive in fence posts, but she could barely lift it. She sat the flashlight on the floor and tugged on the long fiberglass handle of the ten-pound hammer. She yanked it out from behind a rake and hoe, both fell to the floor. She held the handle with two hands and began dragging the sledgehammer toward the shed door before deciding there would be no way she would be able to lift it and pound through a wall.

She dropped it and picked up the flashlight. She shined the light at the ax. Already out of breath, she grabbed its smooth wooden handle with one hand and dragged it to the door. It was heavy, but not as heavy as the sledgehammer. This should get through the wall, she thought as she walked out of the outbuilding, dragging the sharp blade behind her. Then she picked it up with both hands, even with the flashlight in one hand. Then she walked down the gravel path and across the damp grass toward the dark building.

She was breathing heavy by the time she reached the front steps. She stopped when she noticed a single raven perched on the far railing, watching her. She shined her light back and forth along the porch, looking for more of the stocky black birds, or the thing that was following her.

"Shoo, get out of here," she said. Her words were so muted it seemed as if she was going deaf. Then the bird flapped its wings and left, with barely a sound. Crazy. It was as if she was in a fluid vacuum of sinuous waves.

She climbed the steps and walked through the front entrance, setting the ax down to unlock the vestibule door. Her age was getting the best of her. Instead of carrying the ax, she decided to drag it with one hand, while using the flashlight to light her path with the other. It scraped along the hardwood floors, but she did not care if it left a scratch or not. The place was going to be closing and probably torn down at some point.

When she got to the top of the basement steps, she shouted, "Claudia, I have what we need to break through that wall. It's going to make a racket as I drag it down the steps." And indeed it did, each drop of the sharp metal blade was loud.

When she reached the locker room, she shined the light inside as she dragged the ax into the room. She screamed when she saw Claudia passed out on the floor.

"Claudia," she said, letting go of the ax, its handle smacking against the floor. She ran up to Claudia. "Are you okay?"

Claudia did not answer. Ethel knew it was probably the spirits affecting Claudia, but she could not count out the possibility that she had a heart attack or a stroke. She debated whether to run up to her apartment and call 9-1-1 or to continue what they had started. In her gut, she knew it was the spirits affecting Claudia and that paramedics would not be able to help her; only she could help her. It was more important than ever that she get at least a personal item from Deborah, from 1969, to make the spell effective. If they wanted even the slightest chance to banish her, Bruce, and the psychic vampire from this dimension and send them to Hell where they belonged.

She shook Claudia's shoulder. She was relieved when she began to respond. Then she felt for a carotid pulse on the side of her neck, it was weak, but present. She got under Claudia's shoulder and moved her toward the door so that she could begin slashing away at the back wall.

Claudia moaned, and then said, "What are you doing?"

Ethel stopped pulling Claudia when she reached a safe distance from potential flying debris. "Thank God you're okay. What happened?"

Claudia tried to sit up, but she was weak. "Help me sit up."

Ethel helped Claudia sit up and lean against the wall next to the door. All the while Claudia complained about Ethel being too rough or moving her too fast.

Ethel stood and looked down at Claudia. "What happened?"

"After you left to get a hammer I heard two sets of footsteps coming down to the basement. I knew it wasn't you; it was those two spirits. They tried to kill me." She brushed dirt from her arms and began rubbing a sore elbow. "My body may be weak, but my soul is strong."

"Did they say anything?" Ethel asked, shining the flashlight over Claudia. She noticed the elbow Claudia was rubbing was bleeding. She knelt down and took a closer look. "Stop rubbing your elbow, you have a skin tear. We'll dress it when we get back to my apartment."

Claudia pulled her blood-stained hand away. "It was a man and woman and they wanted me to mind my own business. Then the lights went out."

"Let's get the things we need from the lockers and then get back upstairs," Ethel said, dragging the ax to the back of the room. "Then when you're patched up, we'll come back down, get the crystal ball, and begin the séance."

Claudia grumbled. "I just want to get this over with."

Ethel mustered all the strength she could, lifted the ax and swung at the drywall. The steel blade broke through the sheetrock, leaving a small incision.

"Come on, Ethel girl, you can do it," she said aloud. Her breathing was heavy as she lifted the ax and swung again, this time puncturing a bigger slit, creating a hole. It was hollow behind the sheetrock because the ax blade did not contact the back wall as she continued slashing. She repeatedly swung, until she had a hole big enough to work with.

She moved swiftly to the hole and began tearing away at it with her bare hands. Speckles of red blood dotted the white pieces as she ripped them from the wall and let them fall to the floor.

When she had a large hole ripped from the wall, she took the flashlight and looked inside. Yes, it was the rest of the locker room and the lockers were still as they were decades ago.

She picked the ax up once more, and with a loud grunt, she thrust it as hard as she could to tear a larger piece from the wall. The hole in the wall was now big enough to step through. Before she went into the room, she needed to know which locker was Deborah's. Shining the light around she saw that most of the lockers were open and appeared empty, but others were closed and probably locked. She would need the locker list with the locker combinations.

She turned and shined her light at the open file cabinet drawer and then at the folder on the desk next to the extinguished candle. She stepped over the mess she had made and walked up to the desk. The folder tab said: LOCKERS; it was the one she needed. When she looked through the papers inside, she did not see the one she needed. She found copies of the locker room rules, the ones that she handed out to new employees, but not the master combination list.

Then she shined the light at Claudia, still leaning against the doorframe, as if dead. In fact, she looked so much like a corpse that Ethel rushed up to her and knelt at her side, once again feeling for a pulse.

"Stop touching me," Claudia said, pushing Ethel's hand away.

"You looked dead, you old fool," Ethel said, standing up. "Did you find the combination list?"

Claudia removed a partially torn paper from her pocket. "I think it's what you're looking for, the master combination list."

Ethel took the paper and went back to the opening she had hacked away with the ax. She shined the flashlight around the room that had been sealed up for decades. Then she held onto a stud and stepped through. But when she brought her second foot over the bottom of the opening, her moccasin caught on the jagged edge, causing her to stumble forward and fall onto the dingy tile floor. She fell smack on her sore arthritic hip. She let out a cry of pain and grabbed her pelvis with her left hand that was still holding the wrinkled paper. It hurt. It hurt badly. It was the same hip she had fallen on when she tripped over Susie's teddy bear in Maggie's apartment a few months earlier.

Tears streamed from her eyes. She could not believe her luck. She envisioned Detective Becker coming to the apartment Monday morning with the manager to examine the old medical records, only to find two old ladies half dead after demolishing a wall. She laughed and cried at the same time, but at least they would be found.

"Are you all right?" Claudia said, with a high-pitched voice that seemed to make the pain worse.

"It's my hip," Ethel said, wiping tears from her cheeks.

The flashlight had been forced from her hand when she contacted the floor. It had rolled toward the lockers. She turned onto her belly and began sliding across the floor toward the light. Inching her way, her elbows scraping on the floor. She could feel her thin friable skin tear as she moved like a slug toward the light.

Finally, she reached it. It lay with its beam shining at the bottom of the lockers. The toe guard was out of place and she could see underneath the stand of lockers. Then she saw something. She picked up the light and shined the light toward the object. She would need to move the dislodged metal kick plate. Still lying on the floor, she began pulling on the sharp-edged metal with her bloody fingers until she was finally able to move it enough so that she could reach inside. She put her hand through the opening and pulled out an envelope. How had it gotten there? Had it been dropped and accidently kicked underneath, between the tile floor and the metal face, or had someone intentionally hid it there. She opened it and took out a folded letter. It was a letter from Dr. Bruce Hancock addressed to Nurse Deborah. Where were they, by the way? They had attacked Claudia and now she could not sense them. Were they now tormenting Maggie? Probably not, the black-robed entity was likely doing that.

TEN

JESSICA PINTER DREW two draft beers from the tap and sat them on the bar for two unshaven men who would not keep their eyes off her. Normally she liked the attention and encouraged it by wearing low cut shirts that fit snuggly around her breasts, but today she wanted none of it.

Flashers Bar was busy. Football season had begun and patrons were packing the tavern to watch the Sunday games. Boisterous cheers and the smell of grilled burgers filled the air. Typically, she loved the cheerful environment. It was normal for her to end the shift with a jar full of generous tips. Today was different; she wanted to leave, to walk out of the place.

She turned toward the liquor bottles in front of the mirrored wall and looked at her reflection and the barroom behind her.

Everyone was happy except her. She felt sick and for the slightest of moments, she thought she saw a dark cloud around her, but dismissed it as shadows. She had thought there was something following her, just as spirits sometimes follow ghost hunters home. But she was not a ghost hunter. The closest she ever came to a haunted house was Maggie's old apartment at the three-story sanatorium built in 1899, later to become a psychiatric hospital before its final reformation.

The presence she felt had been growing stronger, and today, at this moment, they were exceptionally strong. She knew it was her imagination, after all, but nonetheless she wanted to go home.

She mixed a gin and tonic, took an icy cold beer from the cooler, and sat them on a tray. She picked up the round, brown platter and walked out from behind the bar, to the table where her friends Butch and Junior were watching the game on the big screen TV close to the bar.

"What's wrong with you, Jess?" Butch asked, sounding rather annoyed. His hair, cut in a butch, suited his name well. "You just spilled half my drink on the table."

Jess held the empty tray at her side, dripping from the sloshed around highball cocktail. "Sorry, I'll get you another."

"You look like shit," Junior said, reaching for the brown bottle.

CONNIE MYRES

Typically, Jess would joke back, but today she lashed back instead. "Shut the frickin' hell up."

Jess had planned to quit her waitress job, but Maggie's lawyer, Darron Sugarman, put a hold on funds that should have already been in her possession from Cory's will. The attorney was able to convince the judge that Maggie's husband may have been coerced into changing his will from Maggie as the primary beneficiary, to Jess. Even the distributions from the winning lottery ticket she had taken from Maggie's purse were put on hold. Yes, she was having an affair with Cory, and he was going to divorce Maggie, but he changed his will and committed suicide before Maggie knew what was going on. In Jess's mind, she had done nothing all that wrong; often thinking Maggie deserved it, but she was not sure exactly why.

Suicide. Why did he have to commit suicide? Why couldn't things have gone as planned? She and Cory would be living happily together. But then she thought, maybe I said something. There were times when images from previous blackouts would flash through her mind. She did not like the images, but it was as though she was someone else, doing things a tramp would do. Doing things a . . . not so nice person would do. They were just twisted dreams.

Over a year ago, Jess began drinking heavily. So heavily, that she began having blackouts. She remembered pieces of the things she had done, like the affair with Maggie's husband and the suggestion to him to change his will and divorce Maggie. However, she had no memory of some timeframes. She assumed she had drunk herself into a blackout, only to wake up on her living room floor.

Today she was feeling ashamed of herself, ashamed of what she had done to Maggie. Her best friend, or previous best friend, was now locked away in the psychiatric forensic center and headed to court to face the charge of murdering the apartment superintendent, Mr. Zimmerman.

Jess rubbed her ear; it felt like someone was holding dry ice to it. It itched, burned and was cold. She walked up to the bar and sat her tray on the counter.

"Hank," Jess said when the bartender got in earshot. "I'm going home, I don't feel good."

He turned around and frowned. He was ten years older than she was, but he looked like he was old enough to be her father. His feminine voice seemed out of place coming out of a bulky body. "You can't go home, we're swamped. You have to stay."

"I'll vomit all over everyone, I can't stay. I'm out of here." Jess began walking behind the bar to get her purse, but Hank stopped her.

"I'm not joking," he said, blocking her from reaching under the counter.

She stopped and rubbed her other ear. Both ears were burning as if there were something blowing on them. "I'm not joking either. Move so I can get my things."

"If you leave, don't come back," he said, stepping to the side.

Jess reached under the bar and took her purse. "Don't worry, I quit."

She turned and walked past the table where she had spilled the cocktail.

"Hey, Jess, where's my drink?" Butch said, pissed off.

Jess ignored him and walked out the door.

Jess stopped at the liquor store on her way back to Cedar Creek Trailer Park where she lived. She had planned to be out of the dump by now, but the jewelry she took from Maggie's safe was not easy to sell. She was no better off now than before taking them.

She pulled into her driveway, took the paper bag of liquor off the seat, and went into her house trailer. She closed and locked the door, opened the bottle of spiced gin and took two big gulps. She plopped onto the couch, stained from the drinks she had previously spilled on it.

Her ears continued to itch and burn. Was someone talking about her, like how the old wives tale says? She sensed a presence; the ghosts she felt had been following her.

She sobbed and drank until the pain eased. Then it occurred to her that there was one more item that she had taken from Maggie's safe—Cory's handgun and ammunition.

"Why am I thinking of the gun?" Jess said aloud for no one except her drunken self to hear.

Nevertheless, she got up, went to her bedroom, and took the gun from the back of her closet where she had it hid. She took both the handgun and the box of full metal jacket bullets into the living room. She sat them on the coffee table and took another swig of the gin.

It had grown dark outside while she drank herself into a stupor. She saw her neighbors turn on their porch lights and she could hear people commenting about how it was getting dark so early. She turned her attention back to the gun. She leaned forward, took an FMJ bullet out of the box, and loaded the gun. Then she released the safety and leaned back on the couch, resting the gun on her lap.

A few more swallows and she would have the bottle nearly empty. She had never drunk this much, this fast. She wanted to make the flashbacks go away. They were fading, but there were more. More than she ever wanted to see.

Her ears felt as if they were on fire, she wanted to rip them off. Murmurs in her ears, someone actually was speaking to her. Then one more flashback came to her, a horrible unforgivable deed. She raised the gun to her temple.

ELEVEN

"EVERYBODY UP, EVERYBODY down, it's snack time," the guard said over the loudspeaker.

It was Sunday and the patients were allowed to be in their rooms in the early evening, and that was exactly where Maggie was. Lying on her bed as her heart raced. She could feel something was wrong, the pressure, the weight upon her. She did not want to get up, let alone a snack consisting of a peanut butter sandwich and an orange.

She lay motionless, feeling pinned to the bed. It was as if she were in a sleep paralysis where she could hear the usual sounds of the evening—a patient reading the Bible aloud while others walked around.

Her neck ached, she wanted to die. If she had a gun, she would take her own life, just like Cory. She could not shake the feeling of impending doom. Not only for herself, but also for her best friend Jess—well, former best friend. And for Ethel, especially Ethel. The feeling was overwhelming and unbearable. She could not open her eyes, speak or move, but she could hear everything that was going on around her.

Then there was a screech at her door. Chloe began screaming so loudly it was as though someone was about to behead her with a machete.

"Get off of her," Chloe shouted from the doorway with a loud piercing cry.

Moments later guards were in the room.

"What's going on?" one guard said to Chloe, who now stood mute with her hands over her mouth.

"I'm talking to you, Ms. Ackerman," the guard said, sternly.

"I . . . I see something on Maggie," she said, pointing toward Maggie's motionless body.

"There's nothing on her," the guard said, walking up to Maggie.

One guard began shaking Maggie's shoulder. "Ms. McGee, get up. It's almost time for the med pass."

Chloe ran down the hall shouting, "Don't go down there or the devil will get you."

Maggie opened her eyes and began yelling so loudly her voice began to crack. She began swinging her arms, trying to push away what she thought was the black-robed entity, but instead she was pushing away the guards. She was fighting, screaming, and in a panic. One guard radioed for help while they tried to subdue her, she wanted to run down the hall just as Chloe did, but the guards restrained her.

"Get it away from me," Maggie shouted, struggling against the guards.

Soon another guard arrived with a straightjacket. "Ms. McGee, if you don't calm down you'll need to go to the quiet room." He held up the straightjacket for her to see.

Maggie could not help herself. How could she? The entity fed on her agony every chance it could. She could not escape it, and no one, except Chloe, could see it. Maggie was out of her mind as she kicked at the guards' legs. She wanted to run away, but they would not let her.

Soon, the three guards had her in the straightjacket as they pulled her down the hallway, down the staircase, and through the dayroom to the quiet room, screaming the whole way.

"The demon keeps biting me, it's like a vampire," Maggie yelled. "Somebody has to stop it or I'll die. It's getting stronger."

"There's no demon, Ms. McGee," the guard said, tightening his grip on Maggie's restrained arm.

With the guards still holding her, the nurse gave her an injection of lorazepam to quiet and calm her down. It worked. Soon she was lying on her side on the floor mat.

Maggie heard the door to the room close. Her rapid breaths became quiet as she lay there under the influence of the tranquilizing effects of the benzodiazepine.

A guard stood outside the closed door and looked through the door's shatterproof window. He turned toward the nurse who had just given the injection. "She and Chloe are giving me the heebie-jeebies with all their talk of demons."

Beth, the nurse, dropped the needle into the sharps container. "Yeah, I know what you mean, Wade. But you know there is no such thing as demons and devils."

Wade looked at Beth's trembling hands and smiled. "You don't seem too convinced."

Beth shoved her hands into her blue scrub pants pockets. "There are some people that think mental illness can be caused by demon possession, but I'm not one of them."

Wade nodded and looked back through the window. "Did you see that?"

"See what?" Beth said, moving next to the guard so that she could get a better look into the quiet room.

"Don't report me; I don't want anyone thinking I'm crazy," Wade said. "But I thought I just saw the hair on the side of her neck move as if it was pushed away."

"It probably just fell to the side from gravity," Beth said.

Wade raised an eyebrow. "She kept saying a vampire was biting her neck."

"Are you trying to say there's an invisible vampire in there with her right now?" Beth said. "She's crazy, not a victim of a vampire. You know that."

The guard shrugged. "Yeah, that's totally ridiculous."

Beth walked back to the medication room to continue the evening med pass while Wade kept peering into Maggie's locked room. He kept looking at her, at her hair, at her neck. He rubbed his eyes and looked again. For a moment, it looked like the skin on the side of her neck was moving. Must just be her heart beating.

After Chloe had taken her medication, she looked at Wade, who was looking into the quiet room. She crossed her arms as if a chill had come over her. She timidly walked toward him.

Wade turned and looked at Chloe. "Do you need something, Ms. Ackerman?"

She shrugged a shoulder. "Is Maggie okay?"

Wade nodded. "She's okay. She's sleeping."

Chloe inched slowly closer to the window.

"You need to go back to the day room," Wade said, not wanting Chloe to break out in a screaming rage again.

Very timidly she said, "May I see her?" She looked at the floor and then back up at Wade. "She's my friend; I want to make sure she's okay."

"One quick look and then you need to get back with the others," Wade said, stepping to the side so that Chloe could see inside the white room.

Chloe was taller than Wade and much skinnier. She kept her head down, not yet ready to look into the window. Before she looked up, she asked, "What do you see?"

"Why are you asking me that?" Wade said, annoyed. "I see Ms. McGee lying on her side on the floor."

"Nothing else?" she said.

"What else am I supposed to see?" he said. "You're not afraid of seeing that vampire, are you?"

She looked up at him. "You saw it, didn't you?"

"Don't be ridiculous," Wade said, shaking his head.

Chloe slowly turned her head, and her eyes, to look into the quiet room. She stopped breathing when she saw the dark robed entity wrapped around Maggie with its grotesque head at her neck. Then she saw it look up at her. Chloe could tell that the entity knew she could see it. She held her throat and began gasping for air as she fell into Wade.

"Help, Ackerman's having a seizure," Wade shouted as he lowered the distressed mental patient to the floor.

While the nurse and two other guards came to Chloe's aid, Wade looked back into the quiet room. He saw Maggie's head be yanked back as if someone had pulled it to expose more soft tissue. Then, for a moment, a fleeting moment, he thought he saw a dark shape, with long jagged teeth, bite into Maggie's neck.

Chloe stopped shaking and began weeping as a guard helped her stand. She looked at Wade, who was still looking through the window at Maggie. "You see it, don't you?"

The guard looked at Chloe, who was being escorted away and then at Beth. He wanted to say what he saw, but instead he looked back into the room.

"What's wrong? You look like you saw a ghost," Beth said with a cocked smile.

The guard pointed at Maggie through the window. "Does she look okay to you?"

Beth walked next to Wade and looked through the window at Maggie. "She is laying a little weird, I'll check her. Besides, she can have the restraint removed now."

The guard opened the door for Beth but did not go inside. He watched as she checked Maggie's pulse and respirations. He heard Beth ask Maggie if she was all right and then saw her eyes pop wide open, but she did not say anything. Then he saw the nurse remove the straightjacket and attempt to reposition Maggie's head and body so that she was not so contorted. And that was when he saw the demon inside the room clearly—it was on the mat with Maggie. He saw its black decaying face rise from Maggie's neck and saw its long, snakelike tongue lick some invisible substance from around its mouth. It looked at the nurse and pushed her so hard she hit the wall on the other side of the room. The nurse winced as she slid down to the floor. Then he saw the thing's red eyes look directly at him, and then yank Maggie's head back to expose her neck, and began feeding again. Wade could sense its arrogance and imagined it saying, "So what are you going to do about it, Wadey boy?"

He ran in to help Beth up, but she was already standing and running to the door.

"What the frickin' hell just happened?" Beth said, terrified.

"I don't know," Wade said closing and locking the door. "But it wasn't McGee that pushed you."

TWELVE

OH, THE PAIN in her hip, it was almost unbearable. However, it did not prevent her from shining the light on the yellowed musty page as a mouse scurried underneath the lockers where she had just removed the letter. She shoved the envelope into her skirt pocket and shined the light on the sheet of paper with the locker assignments.

"Are you all right, Ethel? You didn't break your hip, did ya?" Claudia's whiney voice seemed unusually muted. "We'll be stranded down here if you did."

"No, it's just my arthritis, it makes everything worse," Ethel said, looking over the list for Deborah's name. Then she heard Claudia grunting. "What are you doing?"

"I'm getting up so that I can go in there and help you," Claudia said, letting curses slip from her tongue.

Ethel tried to sit up, but every time the hip joint moved a jolt of pain shot down through her leg and up her back.

Claudia stepped between the studs and through the opening. "Did you find the locker?"

"Gosh, this brings back memories," Ethel said as Claudia helped her stand. She shined her light from the paper to locker 41. "That apparently was Patty's locker. I liked her. She was one of the night nurses; she was always leaving as I was coming to work. She'd tell me about the night's events, both terrible and funny."

"Save memory lane for later," Claudia said, looking back through the opening, "because those spirits could return at any moment."

Ethel looked back at the list. "I'm sure her name was Deborah Franklin, but there's no one by that name included in the Fs. There's Joyce Fish, Carrie Fry, but no Franklin."

Claudia walked up to the closed lockers and began trying to open them. Some were locked and some were not. The ones that opened were empty, their contents long ago cleared.

Ethel flipped the paper over and looked at the names on the back. "I don't see her name at all."

"Maybe she didn't have a locker, maybe she shared one with someone else," Claudia said. "What about that doctor? Did he have a locker?"

"I don't know," Ethel said. She was so frustrated she felt like crinkling the paper and tossing it into a corner housing a spider's snare. "I didn't handle the doctor's affairs. But the doctors lounge is on the third floor, the same floor Mr. Zimmerman was . . . murdered."

"Let's check all these lockers first before we go up there," Claudia said, shuffling her edematous feet along the floor, avoiding debris that had been scattered from Ethel's forceful entry.

With flashlight in hand, they looked in all the open lockers and tested each closed one. All they saw in the lockers were trash, old food wrappers, pens—likely depleted of ink—and two pairs of white nurses' shoes, worn and scuffed.

"I can't believe we went through all this and came out empty handed," Ethel said, wincing each time she moved.

"We do have a few cuts and scrapes to show for our hard work," Claudia said, rubbing her elbow. "You'll need to light my path. Let's get back to your apartment."

Ethel shined the light so that Claudia could see to walk back out through the opening. "Maybe we should get the crystal ball while we're down here and take it back to my apartment."

Claudia stopped and turned to Ethel. "It's not wise to take it to your place, you know that. It's best kept in the scrying room until we're ready to use it."

"We could use it now," Ethel said, walking out of the storage room. "Even though we don't have any personal items from the spirits past lives, we can still do it."

"I didn't come all the way here and go through all this just to half-ass the séance," Claudia said. "All we'll end up doing is pissing off the spirits and the demon. We need a personal item from that nurse or the doctor."

"I know," Ethel said. "But I just want to get this over with."

"Nobody wants to get his over with more than me," Claudia said, stamping her cane on the floor. "I want to get this done and get the hell out of this house of horrors. Let's get back to your apartment, strengthen our protection . . . and get a stiff drink."

The two old women hobbled to the steps, moaning and groaning as they climbed them slowly, one by one. When they finally reached the lobby, they heard giggling coming from the second floor. They ignored it as they moved like Weebles that wobble—but these Weebles do fall down.

When they reached Ethel's apartment, she reached into her pocket to unlock the door. "Oh shit, the keys are gone. They must've come out of my pocket when I fell."

"You've got to be kidding," Claudia said with a huff. "Now what?"

"I can either go back down into that room or maybe," Ethel said, holding her left hip as she limped to Mr. Zimmerman's office. "Maybe there's a spare key in there."

"This just keeps getting better," Claudia said, following her.

Ethel tried the door; it was locked. The office had large glass windows on two walls. "I'm going to break into the office."

"They'll be carting us off to jail by the time we're done with this," Claudia said.

Ethel looked at the wooden chair sitting next to the office and then she shined her light toward Claudia. "This glass is old and thin, I should be able to break it."

"Just like us, minus the thin part," Claudia said.

Ethel handed Claudia the flashlight and then picked up the chair. She picked up the ladder-back, turned its legs to face the large pane of glass in the door, and threw it. The side chair bounced off and crashed to the floor, it sounded like she had broken the chair rather than the glass. "I'm trying it again."

"I must say," Claudia said, shining the light so that Ethel could see to throw the piece of furniture again. "You're making this a rather entertaining evening."

Ethel picked up the chair, and instead of throwing it, she held it tight and slammed it into the glass, just as she did the ax in the basement. The glass shattered and spilled to the floor, leaving shards as slippery as ice cubes.

"Are you okay?" Claudia shouted.

"Besides my aching hip, sore back, and bruised elbows," Ethel said, taking the flashlight from Claudia. "I'm fine."

"Can you get in?" Claudia asked.

Ethel walked up to the broken window and used the butt of the flashlight to break the remaining sharp edges so that she could reach through and unlock the door.

Once inside she flipped on the light switch. The new manager must have made sure that, at the very least, the lights worked in Ethel's apartment and in the office. When her light caught the black-and-white picture of Mr. Zimmerman's father, Captain Carl Zimmerman, on his fishing boat with the name Castaway painted on the side, she felt sad. Sad that both these men died in tragic ways. The father died when his boat exploded, and the son died from repeated stab wounds.

She refocused and found a ring of keys in the desk drawer. She knew one had to be a master key that Mr. Zimmerman would use if he ever needed to get into an apartment.

Ethel walked out of the office, briefly shining her light toward the steps leading to the second floor. She was relieved when she saw nothing coming down after them, especially since the giggling had stopped.

She and Claudia walked back to her apartment door, and after trying a few keys, she finally found the one that opened it. Both women rushed inside, closing and locking the door behind them. They stood a moment staring at each other, before each one slowly lowered their sore bodies onto the sofa, one on each side. Ethel flinched with each bend of her hip before she found a comfortable or at least tolerable position. She took a wood tip cigar from the box on the end table and lit it with her bloodstained hands.

"I need a drink," Claudia said, "but I'm too sore and too tired to get up."

"Back before this place got the best of us, back before 1969," Ethel said, sparking a flame, "we were quite the lookers. Now look at us. A couple old witches."

"Speak for yourself," Claudia said, scooting forward so that she could more easily stand. "I'm still a looker."

Ethel laughed. "In your own mind."

Claudia limped to the kitchen and returned with a glass of whiskey in one hand and her cane for support in the other. She sat the liquor on the coffee table before reclaiming her spot on the couch. "I say no more looking tonight. Let's wait until the sun is shining brightly tomorrow and we can actually see what we're doing."

Ethel nodded, and then she remembered the black fog outside the building and its sound muting quality. "If the sun comes out tomorrow."

Claudia took a sip of the biting amber liquid. "Oh, yeah, I forgot about the black cloud hanging over this damned place. Nevertheless, I need rest and so do you."

Ethel took another puff of her thin cigar and blew the smoke toward the ceiling. "There's one problem with waiting."

"What's that?"

"The detective is coming out here tomorrow with the manager to go through the old medical records left behind, looking for information about the murder knife." Ethel took another drag. "And we've trashed the place. How are we going to explain it without being charged with vandalism?"

"So are you thinking we have to go up to the third floor tonight?" Claudia swung her swollen legs onto the coffee table and pulled her knee high compression hose taught. They were wrinkling and cutting into her swollen ankles.

"If we do it tonight and find what we need, we'll be done with the séance by the time Detective Becker and Tim Chandler get here in the morning," Ethel said. "We'll send the demon, Deborah, and Bruce to Hell—God can decide what to do with Susie—and then finish by casting a spell so that we don't go to jail." Ethel lowered her voice and shook her head. "I don't think I'd survive jail."

"A hot bath and a soft bed sound better," Claudia said. "But I suppose us two ragged hags had better finish what we started, and the sooner, the better."

Ethel went to stand but could not move, her damaged hip would not allow her. "But, on the other hand, I think I'd better take some

CONNIE MYRES

pain pills, relax in that hot tub you were talking about, and we'll finish things up tomorrow."

"You're wishy-washy," Claudia said.

"Can you get my pain pills for me," Ethel said, grimacing.

Claudia sighed. "Why didn't you tell me while I was up?"

"I didn't think the pain was going to be this bad," Ethel said, still holding her left hip. "Besides, I don't have a choice. I can't get up, I can barely move."

Claudia finished the distilled spirit in her glass. "I need another drink anyway."

THIRTEEN

TIM CHANDLER WAS walking around the exterior of Sand Piper Bluff Apartments, appearing to be inspecting the foundation, when Det. John Becker drove his Ford Police Interceptor sedan into the parking lot. He got out of the black unmarked police car just as the new building manager stopped his inspection and walked across the uncut grass to meet him.

"I'm Tim Chandler, the new apartment superintendent," the young clean-cut man said, extending his hand.

Det. Becker shook his hand. "I'm Detective Becker, pleased to meet you."

"I don't know what you'll find in those old records," Tim Chandler said, turning to walk toward the sidewalk. "I've never gone through them, of course. Mr. Zimmerman kept them locked in the basement. I guess when they closed the hospital down they just left things that had no other place to go. Moreover, by the looks of the basement, no one has gone down there much except to use the laundry room and tend to the furnace."

Det. Becker followed Mr. Chandler up the porch steps. He looked along its length and at the decaying floorboards. Then he looked out over the landscape where a thick fog was obscuring the forest and the morning sun. "Is it usually this foggy?"

"No, it's not," Mr. Chandler said as he opened the door and stepped into the vestibule. "And I apologize for the condition of the building. When our only tenant moves out, we'll probably end up demolishing the place, for safety reasons, and then sell the vacant land as lakeshore property."

"I can tell this used to be a grand place at one time," Det. Becker said, following Mr. Chandler into the lobby.

Tim Chandler stopped in his tracks when he saw the broken glass, from the office door, scattered over the floor. "What happened here?"

"It looks like someone broke into your office," Det. Becker said, walking up to the office. "Is there anything missing?"

Tim Chandler cautiously stepped over the shards of broken glass and walked to his desk. He looked at the desktop and then began going through the drawers. "The master keys are missing. Someone stole the keys."

"Are the master keys for the apartments in this building?" Det. Becker asked, looking down the hallway toward Ethel's apartment.

"Yeah, they open all the rooms," Tim Chandler said, picking up the flashlight sitting on the desk. "But who would take the keys? There's no reason to go into any of the apartments."

"Is the building kept locked at all times?" the detective asked.

"Yes," Tim Chandler said. "Both the front and back doors require a key to get in and the tenant, Ethel Dory, is currently the only one with a key, besides me, to unlock those doors."

"Was the front door locked when you got here?" Det. Becker asked, looking at the front door and then at the wooden chair laying on its side on top of the glass.

"Yeah, the front door was locked when I got here," Tim Chandler said, walking out of the office. "I'll see if the back door is still locked."

While Tim Chandler walked past Ethel's apartment to check the back door, Det. Becker checked the lower-level windows for any signs of breaking and entering.

"This door is locked, too," Tim Chandler said, walking back to the lobby. "I walked around the building before you got here and didn't notice any tampering with the basement windows, but I must say, they're not in the greatest condition."

"Do you mind if we check the basement?" Det. Becker said, looking toward the dark staircase.

"Sure," Tim Chandler said, switching on his flashlight. "The building's been having electrical problems and the basement lights work only when they want to work."

Det. Becker took a penlight from his breast pocket. "Lead the way, Mr. Chandler."

"You can call me, Tim," he said, walking toward the stairs. He flipped on a light switch near the stairs before walking down the steps. The basement lights powered on. He turned to Detective Becker. "I guess they decided to work today."

They walked down the steps and into the basement. The stench of a rotting rodent filled the air.

"I put out mouse poison," Tim said. "I guess it's doing its job."

"Not a problem," Det. Becker said, looking down the corridor as the lights flickered.

"The records are this way," Tim said, walking down the hallway. He took a key from his pocket and unlocked the door.

"Good thing you brought the key to this room since the ones in the office are missing," Det. Becker said.

"The key to this room wasn't on that ring," Tim said. "Since this room contains old medical records the key was kept with the property manager, Phil Morgan, and not with Mr. Zimmerman's master keys."

"I'll speak with Ms. Dory about the office and the keys before we leave," Det. Becker said walking in behind Tim as he fumbled for the light switch.

They brushed cobwebs away from their faces as they walked into the musty room. Metal file cabinets, boxes of papers, and old charts—still lined up in the rolling chart rack—packed the small space.

"This is my first time in here, Detective. Actually, this is the first time anyone has been in here for years, at least according to Phil." Tim said. "Is there anything I can help you find?"

Det. Becker walked up to the first file cabinet. "I'm looking for records that date back to 1969 when the place closed." He opened the top drawer. "Specifically, records of the murder that occurred at that time and the name of the patient Susan Knight."

"Murder?" Tim said, snorting with surprise. "I didn't know there was a murder here. What happened?"

Det. Becker shined his light on the files in the cabinet and said, "A psychiatric patient murdered an orderly."

"Are you trying to solve a cold case?" Tim said, flipping through a stack of papers inside a cardboard box.

"Something like that," Det. Becker said, pulling out folders to inspect.

While the fluorescent lights in the hallway hummed with a headache-inducing buzz, they went through the documents. They each sneezed from the dust as they found a place to set so they could look through the documents in the dank room.

"Susan Knight," Tim said, taking a folder from the bottom of a box. Inside were off colored papers secured with fasteners. "Is that what you're looking for?"

Det. Becker took the papers from Tim, brushed the dust from the top sheet and began flipping through the pages, each dated and signed by nurses. "These appear to be the nurses' notes from the correct time period. Do you mind if I take these back to the station so that I can take a better look at them?"

"You can take whatever you want, Detective," Tim said. "Like I said, as soon as Ms. Dory moves out of this place it will likely be leveled, and everything in it."

"Thank you," Det. Becker said, flipping through the stack.

"Here are some more papers for Susan Knight," Tim said, picking up another stack of papers that were pinned together. He blew dust and a long dead spider from them and promptly sneezed. "A doctor must have written these because I can't read the handwriting. Now I know why they began making doctors type their notes into a computer."

Det. Becker laughed as Tim handed him the papers. "These are the doctors' progress notes and orders. I think I have what I need."

"Good luck reading that chicken scratch," Tim said.

Then a loud bang echoed through the basement. It was so loud it felt like the whole building vibrated.

"What was that?" Det. Becker asked, walking into the hallway.

"I don't know," Tim said. "I'd say it could be the furnace, but the furnace is off for the summer. It could be the building shifting. I didn't notice a flaw in the foundation, but that doesn't mean there isn't one."

The hallway lights powered off and then back on. Tim shined his light down the hall as he walked to the next room, the room that Ethel and Claudia were in the day before. "What the heck. Someone tore this place apart, too. Looks like they took an ax and broke through the back wall."

Det. Becker walked inside and shined his light through the opening that Ethel had made. "It looks like whoever did this knew there was another room behind the back wall."

"A locker room," Tim said, walking up to it. He stepped inside. "These must be lockers from when this was a working hospital."

Det. Becker's light caught a reflection of something on the floor. He stepped inside and knelt next to a ring of three keys. "It looks like whoever broke in here lost their keys. They're shiny and not covered in dirt like everything else, so they were recently dropped."

Tim bent over to get a closer look. "I know those keys. That one is an apartment key for the first floor and the other is the key to get into the building." He stood up and looked at Det. Becker. "They have to be Ms. Dory's keys. But why would she break in here?"

Det. Becker picked up the keys. "I may have an idea. It also explains why the master keys were taken."

"Ms. Dory is a little eccentric," Tim said, walking back through the opening. "But I'm surprised she did this."

Det. Becker walked through the opening and looked at the open file cabinet drawer, just as the basement lights flickered and then went out. "She was looking for something. I'll go speak with her."

"Watch your step, Detective," Tim said, walking into the dark hallway. "I'm going to check the other rooms. That bang was not normal."

Det. Becker, with stacks of papers and Ethel's keys in his hands, followed Tim as he checked the other rooms. When he got to the scrying room, he pushed open the door, it squeaked as if they were moving a large door in a castle dungeon.

"Detective, look at this," Tim said. He stood at the door and shined his light into the room. "Have you ever seen a room like this before?"

Det. Becker looked into the black room and at the round table with symbols carved into its top. Symbols of the Zodiac were in the outermost perimeter circle, followed by the alphabet, numbers, more symbols, and finally ending with a pentagram in the center. A spent candle sat in the middle. Then he looked at the large mirror on the back wall. It reflected their lights and bodies, but in a muted way, as if a haze was over the glass. Remembering what Ethel had told him, he said, "I think this is a scrying room."

"You mean they had séances in this room?" Tim said, not wanting to explore the room any further.

"Maybe," Detective Becker said, puzzling over their abnormal reflection in the mirror.

Tim walked out of the room and backed away from the door. "That room gives me the creeps. I'm moving on to the laundry room; it has to be a little more reasonable there."

After they had finished inspecting the laundry and furnace rooms, the old kitchen, and archaic wash area, they went back upstairs.

"I'll speak with Ms. Dory then we'll file a police report, if you like," Det. Becker said.

Tim shrugged. "If she pays for the damage done, I won't file a police report."

Det. Becker nodded and walked to Ethel's apartment. He knocked. Moments later Ethel opened the door.

"Oh, hi, Detective," Ethel said, standing off kilter. "Please, come in."

"Thank you." Det. Becker said, walking into Ethel's apartment. He saw Claudia walk out of the bathroom, limping with her cane.

"Detective," Ethel said, staggering to the couch, "this is my friend Claudia. Claudia this is Detective Becker."

"Nice to meet you, ma'am," Det. Becker said, nodding with a smile.

Claudia looked at the papers that Detective Becker was carrying and then sat at the opposite end of the sofa as Ethel. "Looks like you've been in the basement."

"Yes, I have, and it appears that someone has broken through a wall in one of the rooms, and also into the superintendent's office. Would you happen to know anything about that?"

"Would you like a cup of coffee, Detective?" Ethel asked, sweetly.

"No, thank you."

Ethel looked at Claudia and then at Det. Becker. "I must confess, Detective, that I did both deeds. Claudia and I were looking for information that could help save Maggie. She's innocent and I just need some physical proof to keep her from going to prison."

"I'm glad you admitted to the damages," Det. Becker said. "Tim Chandler said that if you pay for the damages that he won't press charges."

"He's such a kind young fellow," Ethel said. "Of course, I'll pay for the damages."

Detective Becker held up the set of keys. "Do you know who these belong to."

Ethel winced. "They're mine. They came out of my pocket when I fell and hurt my hip. That's why I had to break into the office; I needed to get into my apartment without having to go back down into that room."

Det. Becker looked at the two feeble old women. He felt like explaining the law to them but he knew they already knew it, or at least knew it well enough to know what they did was not legal. He also knew that the building would be torn down soon and that her intent was to help Maggie, not vandalize. Then he wondered if they had found what they were looking for. "Did you find anything?"

Ethel looked at the papers in his arms. "I see you have." She looked at the envelope sitting unopened on the coffee table, unsure whether to tell him she found it or not because she wanted to read it before she let it leave her possession. She would have read it already but last night the pain pills put her to sleep and this morning she only just woke up when she heard the detective knocking on her door. On the other hand, Det. Becker was being lenient with her and the mess she made of the apartment building. She groaned in pain as she reached for the letter. "I found this letter, but I haven't read it yet."

"Where did you find it?" Det. Becker asked.

Ethel began opening the envelope. "You may as well set down, Detective; I'd like to read this before you take it . . . if that's all right." She pulled the brittle piece of notepaper from the envelope. "When I fell I noticed this underneath the lockers."

The detective walked over to the round table in the living room and sat the stack of

CONNIE MYRES

papers on it. He sat down, and said, "Could you read it aloud, please?"

"Sure, Detective," Ethel said, putting on her reading glasses. "The envelope is addressed to Deborah Franklin and is from Dr. Bruce Hancock."

"What date is on the postmark?" Det. Becker asked.

Ethel looked at the envelope. "It is dated September 11, 1969."

"Is that when the hospital closed?" Claudia asked. Her voice was so shrill; Det. Becker immediately looked at her.

"Sometime around there," Ethel said, unfolding the paper.

"Was the envelope sealed when you found it?" Det. Becker asked.

"No, it wasn't," Ethel said. "It had been opened."

"May I have the letter and envelope when you're done reading it?" Det. Becker asked.

"Whatever you like, Detective," Ethel said. Then with a gravelly voice, she began:

"Deborah, I am writing you this letter because I did not want to be seen speaking with you, especially about Susan Knight.

First, I know you charted that the patient used bandage scissors to kill the orderly. I just do not want you to forget and chart or say otherwise.

Second, don't mention that you and I saw the knife that Dr. Suharto brought to the hospital. . . ."

Ethel stopped and looked up at the detective. "Doctor Suharto? That's the same name as Maggie's psychiatrist."

Det. Becker nodded in agreement. "Please continue reading."

Ethel looked back down at the paper.

"Dr. Suharto quickly hid the knife after the incident and is prepared to deny its existence. He is a good doctor and I do not want his career to end over this, he will offer much great healing and benefit to psychiatric patients wherever he ends up taking residence.

Thank you for helping the young doctor remove the knife and replace it with bandage scissors. Susan Knight would have murdered the orderly with the scissors, or whatever weapon was handy, so there is no need to speak of the knife.

The doctor's grave error in carrying the knife in his lab coat pocket instead of replacing in his briefcase was a bad decision. However, as you know, he was responding to a medical emergency. And because he has the utmost concern for the patients, he rushed to Susan Knight's bedside to help her, not hurt her or the orderly.

CONNIE MYRES

One last thing. Since the knife was bloody
and people were all around, he wrapped it in
a towel and hid it behind . . ."

Ethel looked up. "The page is ripped."

"May I see it," Det. Becker said, reaching for it.

"Could the knife be the same one that was found in Maggie's laundry?" Ethel asked, grasping at any straw she could.

"If it's been hidden here in this building all this time," Claudia said, as she kicked off her slip-on shoes. "Who would know about it?"

"The spirits know about it," Ethel said. "Deborah and Bruce would know. And that Doctor Suharto would know."

"But why would Doctor Suharto murder Mr. Zimmerman and frame Maggie?" Claudia put her massive legs on the coffee table.

"I still say the spirits had something to do with it," Ethel said.

"I agree with Ethel, Detective," Claudia said. "There are spirits here. I was the medium who accidently summoned the demon into the building, into this world, back in 1969. Down in the basement, in the scrying room."

"Ms. Dory," Det. Becker said. "Who else has been in this building, recently, besides you, Ms. McGee, Mr. Zimmerman, and the new manager?"

"No one," Ethel said, folding the letter and placing it back into the envelope. "It's been only me and Mr. Zimmerman for a long time."

"Until Ms. McGee moved in," Det. Becker said, standing up. He picked up the stack of papers and the letter. "I'll be in touch," he said, walking to the door. Then he stopped and turned to Ethel. "Don't forget to settle up with Tim Chandler. And you two ladies stay out of trouble."

Ethel smiled and briefly fluttered her scant eyelashes as he walked out the door.

Claudia turned to Ethel. "Where do you think that doctor hid the knife?"

"I don't know," Ethel said. "But I'm getting the feeling it was in the scrying room."

"You talked to him a couple days ago, didn't you?" Claudia said. "Did you talk about the knife?"

"Yes, I did talk with him," Ethel said. "But I don't think we talked about the actual murder or the knife."

"Do you think that Maggie's doctor is the same Doctor Suharto that was in the letter?" Claudia asked.

"I don't know. I'm sure there is more than one psychiatrist named Suharto," Ethel said, standing and limping to the phone. "But there's one way to find out."

"Who are you calling?" Claudia asked.

"I'm calling Doctor Suharto," Ethel said, taking a business card held to the face of the refrigerator by a magnet. "I'm going to bait him."

"How?" Claudia said.

"I'm going to tell him details about the knife, or rather the karambit as the detective calls it and see if I can make him wonder if it's the same knife as the one he hid," Ethel said. "I'll mention something about the DNA testing being done on it. Because if it is the same knife, his DNA may be on it and maybe he'll take the bait and come here and see if his knife is still in its hiding place."

"You can also mention that they're going to be tearing down the building," Claudia said. "He won't want the knife being found in the building's debris. But even if it is the same knife, it doesn't mean that he killed Mr. Zimmerman. He probably didn't even know Mr. Zimmerman."

"Actually," Ethel said. "I doubt Doctor Suharto murdered Mr. Zimmerman, it makes no sense. But what I'm curious about is the knife."

"Why don't you just let the detective take care of it?" Claudia said. "I'm sure he's planning on speaking with the doctor. Plus, it would be easy enough to find out if he worked here in the past because it has to be listed in his work history."

"I want to find the knife that Susan Knight used to kill the orderly," Ethel said. "And I bet it's this Doctor Suharto that hid it."

"And what good will that do?" Claudia asked.

"It'll show that somehow these things are connected," Ethel said. "And more importantly, it may get us closer to finding out who actually murdered Mr. Zimmerman."

Ethel dialed the old rotary phone. It rang to the doctor's office.

"Doctor Suharto's," a female receptionist said.

"May I speak with Doctor Suharto?" Ethel said.

"May I ask whose calling?" the receptionist said.

"This is Ethel Dory, I'm the emergency contact for Margaret McGee and I have some important information for Doctor Suharto."

"He's with a client right now. I could have him call you back," she said. "Oh, wait; the client just left. I'll see if he'll take your call. Can you hold?"

"Yes, I can wait."

While a recording of the history and benefits of Port Glenn Psychiatric and Forensic Hospital played in the background, Ethel waited. She looked at Claudia, who was now walking toward her, wanting to hear what was being said on the phone.

"This is Doctor Suharto. How can I help you?"

Ethel held the phone's receiver so that Claudia could hear. "Hi, Doctor Suharto. This is Ethel Dory, Maggie McGee's emergency contact. I was wondering if you've had a chance to read the police report about Mr. Zimmerman's murder."

"Why do you ask?"

"Because I've talked to the homicide detective in charge of the case and he mentioned a strange kind of knife, he called it a karambit," Ethel said, winking at Claudia. "Have you heard of that kind of knife before?"

"Yes, I have. What is its significance?"

"I'm the only tenant left in Sandpiper Bluff Apartments, the building that used to be Lakeshore Sanatorium and Psychiatric Hospital, decades ago. Anyway, soon as I leave they are going to be setting the wrecking ball to this old building. The detective found old medical records from 1969 with the name Doctor Suharto on them. Do you happen to be related to that doctor?"

Claudia frowned and mouthed 'what are you talking about?'

The doctor did not answer right away and then he said, "It sounds to me, Ms. Dory, that you're trying to conduct your own investigation. If you have any further questions regarding this matter, you can take them to my attorney. Good day."

"He just hung up on me," Ethel said, dropping her jaw.

"You didn't quite tell the doctor the truth," Claudia said. "And you probably just ruined your chance of ever talking to him again."

"I want him to come here and see if his knife is still in its hiding place," Ethel said, shaking a finger because of her keen idea. "By telling him that I'm the only one in the building and that it soon will be demolished, he may come back and look for it."

"How's he getting in?" Claudia said, walking back to the couch.

"I'll leave the front door unlocked," Ethel said, walking into the spare room where Maggie's belongings were kept. She unzipped Maggie's backpack and took out her video camera. "I'll hide the camera, and when he comes here and goes into the scrying room— where I think the knife is, or rather used to be kept until someone took it out and murdered poor Mr. Zimmerman—it'll trip the motion detection sensor on the camera and record him looking for it. The scrying room is the one place people didn't go to every day. I'm sure he didn't want a bloody knife in the doctor's lounge or in his car."

"If he comes here looking for the karambit, it means he didn't murder your superintendent," Claudia said. "All it'll prove is that he is the same Doctor Suharto that worked here in 1969, and the detective can figure that out rather easily."

"And the same Doctor Suharto who covered up murder evidence and saved his career," Ethel said. "And it will show us if the knife is still there, and if it's gone then the karambit that was used to kill Mr. Zimmerman was the same one from 1969."

"It still won't tell us who killed the superintendent. So exactly how does that help Maggie?" Claudia said.

Ethel sighed. "I don't know, but it at least shows there are more people involved than Maggie. And it'll prove that the knife was not one Maggie owned and that more investigation will need to be done before Maggie is sent to prison."

"Okay," Claudia said, as she used the handle of her cane to pull a pillow toward her. "Next, and I really hate to ask this question, but when are we doing that séance? I'm only asking because I want to get it over with so that I can get the hell out of this building and go home and relax where there's no stress."

"Let's reinforce our protection and then do it around noon," Ethel said, fiddling with the camera. "I'm not looking forward to doing it either, but we need to do it to weaken the spirits and hopefully send them and the demon back to Hell."

FOURTEEN

DET. HALEY WANAT sat at her desk across from Det. Becker. "Those papers are so musty I can smell them from here. What are you reading?"

"I'm looking through these medical records from 1969," Det. Becker said, brushing a dry flat centipede from a page. "I'm looking for the blood type of the patient Susan Knight and the orderly that was murdered. I need to see if the karambit used in the Zimmerman murder case is the same one that was used in 1969."

"If it is, how did McGee get it?" Det. Wanat asked, tapping computer keys.

"I don't think McGee got it," he said. "I have a hunch it was someone else."

Wanat looked up from her desk. "Who?"

"I don't know, but I'm going to speak with Doctor Suharto this afternoon," Det.

Becker said, blowing more filth from the pages. "I have Peggy checking to see if the Doctor Suharto from 1969 is the same doctor currently overseeing Ms. McGee's case."

"You don't think the doctor committed the murder, do you?" Det. Wanat said.

"I highly doubt it. But if it is the same weapon, and it was hidden in the building all these years, I think Ms. McGee either found it while she was a tenant there. Or someone else found it and framed her," he said.

"So McGee could still be guilty," Det. Wanat said. "She found it, went nuts, and killed the superintendent."

"It's possible, but there's no motive," Det. Becker said. "Ms. McGee had no reason to murder him, other than the disease she has, schizophrenia, could have made her think he was someone else. Maybe she believed she had to protect herself—a hallucination or delusion from someone not in their right mind. On the other hand, she could have been framed as she has said, but by who and for what reason. I don't think Doctor Suharto framed her."

"What about the ghosts," Det. Wanat said in jest. "Didn't McGee talk about reincarnation and that she was one of the nurses working there in 1969. She even mentioned their names, Deborah somebody and a doctor she called Bruce. She even mentioned the little girl she called Susie, who apparently is Susan Knight. Is it possible that she got into the medical records when she lived there, found their names and the knife, and then went off the deep end and killed Mr. Zimmerman? No reincarnation. No ghosts. Besides, can ghosts even lift things?" Det. Wanat laughed.

"According to the current property manager, Tim Chandler, no one has been in that room in years," Det. Becker said. "And by all the cobwebs, dust, and dirt in the medical records room, that appears to be the case. If Ms. McGee had been in that room, there was no evidence of it."

"Maybe there are more medical records in the building, or maybe the psychic said something to her," Det. Wanat said, leaning back in her chair. "Especially since that Ethel used to work there in 1969. Could she have committed the murder? Maybe she framed McGee. It would be pretty easy to frame a crazy person."

"That is another possibility," Det. Becker said. "Ethel doesn't seem like the type to commit murder, but I've been a detective long enough to know you can't judge a book by its cover."

"To me, the psychic seems to be the most likely suspect," Det. Wanat said. "She knows the history of the building. And she would know the names of the staff without having to go into the medical records room, she may have known where the karambit was hidden, and she knew Mr. Zimmerman a long time. In fact, they were the only ones in the building for quite some time. Maybe they were romantically involved

CONNIE MYRES

and something happened, and the psychic got angry or jealous and wanted revenge and the new tenant, McGee, provided the perfect way to commit the crime. Ethel Dory could even have had a key to McGee's apartment, especially since McGee's apartment still used an old skeleton key. McGee would be easy to setup, especially since her husband just committed suicide and the disease of schizophrenia has apparently been progressing." Det. Wanat clasped her hands behind her head. "This whole mission she has to save McGee could just be a ruse to keep us off track."

Det. Becker had considered the possibility of Ethel Dory being the perpetrator of the crime, but there was no evidence. He had never gotten the sense that she was involved, other than trying to help Maggie. His gut was typically right and he trusted it, but it was not one hundred percent accurate. With Det. Wanat pointing out the obvious, suspicion was shifting from Maggie to Ethel.

"Hey, Becker." Peggy Hernandez said, walking into the criminal investigation room. She laid some papers on his desk. "It looks like it's the same Doctor Suharto. He had a stint of residency at the Lake Shore Sanatorium and Psychiatric Hospital in 1969. Then he moved on to the Kalamazoo Psychiatric Facility and then finally into his position as a primary psychiatrist at Port Glenn Psychiatric and Forensic Hospital."

"Has anything come back on the DNA?" Det. Becker asked as he looked over the paperwork that Peggy had brought in.

"Not yet," Peggy said, putting her hands on her hips.

"I'm going to see if I can get a voluntary cheek swab from Ethel Dory and Doctor Suharto," Det. Becker said. He looked up at Peggy still standing by his desk. "I need to leave soon to speak with the doctor. I'll catch up with Ms. Dory later. Can you go through these documents for me, Peggy?"

"Sure, what am I looking for?" Peggy said.

"First, this letter goes into evidence for the 1969 murder of an orderly named Damian Richards at Lake Shore Sanatorium and Psychiatric Hospital," Det. Becker said. "As far as the rest of these papers, I need evidence that the murder weapon used by a ten-year-old patient named Susan Knight, was covered up. It'll be evident when you read the letter. Also, I need information on the nurses Deborah Franklin and Margaret Austin, including pictures if you can find some. I also need information on Doctor Bruce Hancock, and of course, Doctor Aditya Suharto. And Ethel Dory, she was a receptionist there during the time of the murder. With all the similarities between these people, see if you can find anything out about Mr. Carl Zimmerman. I wouldn't be surprised if he worked there during that time, as well."

"Wow, two murders decades apart with possibly the same weapon and all these people with some connection between the two cases," Peggy said. She held out her hand ready to take the smelly paperwork.

"The pile of papers is all yours," Det. Becker said as he stood. He looked at Det. Wanat. "I'm going to the crime lab to get a couple buccal swab collection kits and then I'm going to see Doctor Suharto, first."

Det. Wanat smiled. "Johnny, you get all the interesting cases."

§ § §

"NICE TO MEET you, Detective Becker," Dr. Suharto said, motioning for the detective to step inside his office. "Please, have a seat."

"Thank you," Det. Becker said, sitting in the same leather chair that Ethel had sat in a couple days earlier.

"You're here about Margaret McGee?" the doctor asked, seated at his desk.

"Yes, I am," Det. Becker said. "Do you mind if I ask you a few questions?"

"Not a problem," Dr. Suharto said. "I have to meet with a client shortly, but I have time to answer a few questions."

"I'll get right to the point," Det. Becker said. "Have you ever worked at Lake Shore Sanatorium and Psychiatric Hospital?"

Dr. Suharto frowned. "I was a resident there while I was going through my medical training. It was a long time ago. Why do you ask?"

"Do you remember any of the doctors, or psychiatrists, that you trained under?" Det. Becker asked.

Dr. Suharto cleared his throat. "Like I said, it was a long time ago, Detective. I've trained under many doctors."

"Does the name Doctor Young ring a bell?" Det. Becker said.

Dr. Suharto shook his head and leaned back in his cushiony desk chair. "No, can't say as though it does."

"How about Doctor Bruce Hancock?"

Dr. Suharto stared at Det. Becker. He leaned forward and looked down at his desk as if he were searching for something. "It sounds familiar."

"Have you read Ms. McGee's police report?" Det. Becker asked.

"Yes, what a sad state of affairs. Ms. McGee was living with undiagnosed schizophrenia, which was made worse by the suicide of husband, and by that . . . if you don't mind my saying . . . that crazy women who calls herself a seer. Did you know, Detective, that she had the nerve to call me earlier today asking if I knew anything about the karambit and wondering if I had worked in her apartment building when it was a hospital? The point, Detective, is that she was insinuating that I had something to do with . . ." he shook his head, "I don't know what.

The woman is essentially conducting her own investigation. Can you do something to stop her from harassing me?"

"I'm sorry," Det. Becker said. He strained to hold back a smile, amused that Ethel was pressuring the doctor. "I'll have a talk with her. I didn't realize she was . . . harassing you."

Dr. Suharto fidgeted with the papers on his desk. "It's just a coincidence that I happened to work at that hospital in the late sixties."

"Did you know the murder victim, Mr. Carl Zimmerman?" Det. Becker asked, watching the doctor intently, assessing his body language and gesture clusters. He could tell the doctor was uncomfortable with the questioning.

The doctor shook his head. "No, it doesn't ring a bell, as you say."

"Do you remember a Mr. Zimmerman working at the hospital and at the same time as you?" Det. Becker said, trying to connect the people with the two murders.

"I don't remember," Dr. Suharto said. He glanced at the detective and then back down at his desk. "I don't think I paid much attention to other staff in the facility."

Det. Becker reached into his pocket and pulled out the photograph of the karambit. "Have you seen this before?"

Dr. Suharto took the photograph, studied it a moment, and then handed it back. "It's a karambit. I hope you're not suggesting that I know anything about the actual murder weapon."

"Just routine questions," Det. Becker said, placing it back into his pocket. "What do you know about karambits?"

"I know it's found in Asia and has been around for hundreds of years," Dr. Suharto said.

"What is your country of origin?" Det. Becker asked.

"Indonesia," Dr. Suharto said, angrily. "Surely, Detective, you're not here to lay the murder of Mr. Zimmerman on me?"

"No, I apologize," Det. Becker said, not wanting to make the doctor defensive and refuse the cheek swab. He held up the cheek swab kit that he had brought in with him. "Would you mind if I performed a buccal swab? It's routine and is voluntary."

Dr. Suharto rolled his eyes. "If I don't allow the buccal swab I'll look guilty, so go ahead, Detective, perform the swab."

Det. Becker had the doctor sign a consent form. Then he put the cotton-tipped applicator into Dr. Suharto's mouth and swabbed the inside of his cheek. Then he placed it into a receptacle with a desiccant and applied the tamper-evident police evidence seals. "Thank you, Doctor Suharto. Your cooperation is greatly appreciated."

FIFTEEN

ETHEL ROLLED UP the floral area rug lying in the middle of her apartment's living room, revealing a five-pointed star painted on the hardwood floor. After the demon was released in 1969, she modified the pentagram to represent the Star of Bethlehem, with each point of the star having a biblical heroine. While Ethel was not a member of the Order of the Eastern Star, she valued the Freemasonic Order and its biblical teachings. Actually, Ethel knew very little about OES, but she hoped that its dedication to charity, truth, and loving kindness would counteract the evil in the building.

She also knew that she was not using the emblem the way it should be used. However, she was a psychic, a crystal gazer, a seer and knew that good trumps evil . . . usually; and wanted all the help she could get.

Claudia lit a blessed white candle on the round table while Ethel retrieved a wooden magic wand from the gold tin box on the shelf containing all her thaumaturgy.

"I can't believe we're waiting until late afternoon to cast the spell of protection," Claudia said, blowing out the match; causing the smell of sulfur to penetrate through the previous sage smudging. "It'll be dark before we know it."

"I had to wait for my pain pills to kick in," Ethel said, limping to the star.

"And we never came up with any personal items," Claudia said. She walked onto the star and stood across from Ethel.

"We'll make due," Ethel said, holding the wand in her hand. Made of elder wood, with carvings of elderberries running down its length, it reminded Ethel of Dumbledore's wand in the Harry Potter movies. She had received it from her great-grandmother Muma, not from the headmaster of Hogwarts Wizarding School.

"Have you even seen the crystal ball, lately?" Claudia asked, wearily supporting herself with her cane.

"No, but I know it's still in the scrying room," Ethel said. "Are you ready?"

"Get on with it already," Claudia grumbled.

Ethel raised the wand toward the ceiling and said:

"Terra, Ignis, Aqua,

All three,

Elements of astral I summon thee.

Earth by Divinity, Divinity by Earth,

Give the enemy the power to see,

The strength of the elements by my side,

No rules magic I shall abide.

Now when my enemy meets his downfall,

This spell will have no power left at all.

In no way shall this spell reverse or place upon me any curse.

So mote it be."

Ethel lowered the wand and closed the circle just as the building began to shake. Knickknacks of small glass potion bottles started to rattle on a shelf while kitchen cupboard doors began to open.

"Let's hurry to the basement while we can," Ethel said, picking up the video camera, a blessed candle, and a small clear bottle of Holy water. She walked to the door and cracked it open. No one was outside waiting for them. "Hurry."

The two old women hobbled down the hallway, past a pile of broken glass that Tim had swept into a corner, and then rushed through the lobby. The building was still shaking as they went down the steps. Claudia lost her footing and slipped, causing her to set her bottom on a step. Ethel helped her stand and they continued down to the basement and its flickering fluorescent lights.

With little time to think, Ethel tucked the programmed video camera between a cinderblock and a loose stone from the original basement foundation. With all the movement, Ethel knew it was recording her endeavors, but that was okay, at least the detective would see what was happening. She pointed it toward the scrying room and ran over to meet Claudia, who was already inside.

"Which panel is it?" Claudia said, pushing on the dark rectangular sections of the walls.

Ethel began pushing on sections of the wood paneling, hoping to release a latch and pop the panel door open. "I think the building is shifting and making it so that the door won't open."

"Find it, and fast," Claudia said, sitting at the round table. She lit the candle that she had brought and held it in place in the center of the witching board carved into the tabletop.

"I got it," Ethel shouted, as a wall panel opened. The building immediately stopped shaking when she touched the quartz crystal ball. She gently lifted the cantaloupe-sized globe, and its stand, with two hands and sat it in front of Claudia. "It's just as beautiful as it was decades ago."

"I'm actually amazed it still shines," Claudia said, placing her hands on the sphere. The light from the candle made it sparkle and glow as if powering on and coming to life.

Ethel kept the scrying room door open so that the camera would record their scrying session and because she did not want to leave the safety of the table. In the lobby above them, tremendous thuds pounded the floor as the basement grew pitch black.

Claudia kept her gaze on the crystal ball. Soon a mist began to form, swirling and swirling inside the orb. Then the images around and inside the crystal ball began to clear and brighten, emitting a white light of protection around them and the table.

A woman's laughter bellowed at the top of the staircase and grew louder as it descended the basement steps. Then Ethel noticed something dark in a far corner of the room. Not a shadow, but something in the shape of a man; a man with a black cloak.

The lenses of Claudia's thick cataract glasses reflected the dancing light from the crystal ball and the candle as she stared into the sphere. She moved her hands gently around the globe as if she were moving soap foam floating on top of bath water toward her.

Ethel shivered, wanting to cross her arms from the frigid air. Instead, she kept her hands on the table and watched Claudia work the crystal. She whispered to her, "The demon is here with us."

"I know," Claudia said, not breaking her gaze from the swirling mist inside the globe. Then with an edgy determination, she said, "Demon Vampire from Hell, what is your name?"

There was no answer. All they heard was the laughter, now at the bottom of the basement steps at the far end of the hall.

"Demon Vampire from Hell, what is your name?" Claudia said again, her whiney voice seeming to contradict the authority she commanded.

A low guttural laugh came from the corner of the room, as it emitted a sense of impending doom.

"I will call you Lamia, demon vampire and will send you back where you came from . . . back through the gates of Hell, along with the evil spirits Deborah Franklin and Bruce Hancock." Claudia said. She was shaking, because of the icy air and from fear of what the demon may do to them.

Spit splattered on the table; a brown glob of sticky mucus. Ethel almost jumped from her seat, but she stayed focused on Claudia, ready to intervene if the demon threatened her.

While the building trembled, causing the witching table to vibrate, Ethel held the glass decanter of Holy water tight. Then she prayed with Claudia:

"Saint Michael the Archangel,

CONNIE MYRES

Defend us in battle.

Be our defense against the wickedness and snares of the Devil.

May God rebuke him, we humbly pray."

The building shook violently, as if ready to topple down upon them, completing its own demolition. Outside the door of the scrying room, Ethel saw Deborah and Bruce. Their faces were contorted and corpselike. Then she slowly turned her head and looked at the black-robed demon now standing behind Claudia. She saw rotten flesh covering its face and maggots wiggling from its hollow eye sockets, falling onto the top of Claudia's head. The demon placed a hand on each side of Claudia's face. Ethel saw its fingers, slime-covered bones, preparing to squeeze Claudia's skull until it popped.

She wanted to grab Claudia and run out of the room, but if she did that, she would give the demon more power; it would know they were weak and that it was strong. She looked at the crystal ball, still filled with a warm white light and continued the prayer with Claudia.

"And do thou,

O Prince of the heavenly hosts,

By the power of God,

Thrust into hell Satan,

And all the evil spirits,

Who prowl about the world

Seeking the ruin of souls. Amen."

When they finished the prayer, asking Saint Michael the Archangel to intercede, she saw the demon lower its head to Claudia's neck, preparing to feed on her life essence, just as it has been doing to Maggie. Ethel uncapped the bottle she held and, as if she were throwing a Frisbee, she doused the demon, Claudia, Deborah, and Bruce with one the Holy water. They cried out in agony and began to sizzle and to smoke. Ethel knew that the searing of the spirits was a sign that the fires of Hell were reaching for them and pulling them down into its flaming pit of anguish. Moments later, they were gone. The smell of burnt meat filled the room as the building creaked and settled onto its shaky foundation.

"Close the door to Hell," Ethel said, holding the nearly empty container of Holy water. "Before they come back through it."

When Claudia finished chanting the spell of closure, the crystal ball went dark and the room warmed.

"Are they in the crystal ball?" Ethel asked, looking at the inky swirls inside the globe.

Claudia brushed the squirming maggots from the top of her head as she rose from the chair and backed away from the table. She stumbled on a fallen ceiling panel and was about to fall backward onto the concrete when Det. Becker caught her from behind.

"What just happened?" Det. Becker said, supporting Claudia until she was standing on her own.

Ethel handed Claudia her cane and smiled. "You came just in time, Detective. We sent the evil spirits back to Hell."

"Are you two all right?" Det. Becker asked, scratching his head.

"I'm fine," Claudia said, walking back to the table. "They almost came back through the door, but I closed it just in time."

Det. Becker walked up to the crystal ball filled with a black substance, like a black Krampus snow globe. At times, he thought he saw glimpses of faces and flashes of fire. He looked next to the globe and saw the maggots wiggling along the tabletop. The atmosphere felt lighter than when he first walked into the building; even the stink of rotting rodents was replaced with a faint scent of roses. "Did you just perform a séance?"

"We did," Ethel said, holding her chin high. "Now the spirits won't bother Maggie, or anyone else for that matter, anymore. We just need to bury the crystal ball and our mission is completed."

"I can see, Detective," Claudia said, walking up next to him. With a squeaky voice of victory, she said, "I see that maybe you are a believer, now."

Det. Becker raised his eyebrows, unsure how to answer. He indeed was seeing things he had never seen before. He looked at the two war-torn elderly women standing before him. He knew they had battled something, but he was unsure exactly what. "You ladies are sure making a believer out of me."

"Can I ask you a favor, Detective," Ethel said, glancing toward the swirling liquid in the globe.

"What do you need?" Det. Becker asked, knowing she was going to ask him for a far-out favor.

"Can you carry the crystal ball up the stairs and out of the building? I fear that if Claudia and I were to try and move it, it would end up shattered on the floor, not to mention the demon and spirits would be released."

Det. Becker glanced at the inky ooze and then back at Ethel. He sighed as he picked up the crystal ball, removing it from its stand as the black ink continued moving inside. "It's cold."

"Be careful with that," Claudia snapped. "I can't go through another séance. It'll kill me."

Det. Becker gently handled the round crystal, following the women up the stairs and out the back door.

"What do you plan on doing with this?" Det. Becker said. He stood on the back porch as the setting sun spewed its golden rays of light over them. The charcoal fog was gone, replaced with the fresh, moist scent of Lake Michigan water gently blowing across the high bluff.

"While Ethel gets the shovel, you and I can find a secret place where it can be buried and not disturbed when then tear down the building," Claudia said, wincing with each painful step she took down the porch steps and onto the tall grass of the back lawn.

"I'm feeling rather foolish carrying this thing," Det. Becker said, following Claudia.

"Take it over there," Claudia said, pointing with her cane not far from the cliff. "By that big rock."

Det. Becker and Claudia walked over to the shoulder-high boulder, long ago deposited by a retreating ice sheet. Soon Ethel returned with a shovel.

"I'll take the crystal ball, Detective," Ethel said, leaning the shovel against the rock. "If you don't mind digging the hole."

Det. Becker sniggered as he handed Ethel the crystal ball and took the shovel. He stuck the point into the ground. "Right here?"

"Perfect," Claudia said, winking at Ethel. "You're a good man."

"I feel like a criminal who's in cahoots on a scheme to hide evidence," Det. Becker said as he pushed the shovel blade into the ground.

"We're not hiding evidence," Ethel said, watching him dig into the hard clay soil. "We're just hiding the crystal ball so that no one will ever find it and release the demon."

Det. Becker did not say anything as he shoveled until he had a hole that he thought was deep enough.

"Dig it deeper, Detective," Claudia demanded. "Because you never know if someone is going to plant flowers around this eyesore, trying to make it beautiful, and I don't want them digging up the gateway to Hell."

"Gateway to Hell? That sounds ominous," Det. Becker said, digging at least three feet down into the earth. He wiped sweat from his brow. "I can't dig any deeper."

Ethel handed him the crystal ball. He placed it carefully into the bottom of the hole and shoveled the dirt over it. Then Ethel packed the dirt down filling the hole with the sole of her moccasin.

When Ethel was finished, she stood back and admired their accomplishment. "I'm surprised you came out today, Detective. Was there something you needed?"

"Actually, I have a few more questions," Det. Becker said, walking onto the porch with the women. He leaned against the porch rail as the two golden agers each sat in a rocking chair. He wiped the remaining soil from his hands and took the notepad and pen from his pocket. "How long did you know Mr. Carl Zimmerman?"

"I've known him for decades, ever since I worked here," Ethel said, rocking back and forth. "He was the janitor here before he was a superintendent."

CONNIE MYRES

"Were you and he romantically involved?" Det. Becker asked, as seriously as he could.

Claudia burst out laughing, thrusting the tip of her cane on the porch. "You're making my day, Detective."

Ethel looked at Claudia and began laughing herself. Then she caught her breath. "Heavens, no, Detective, why would you think that? We were good friends, nothing more."

"You've lived here a long time, have you ever been in the medical records room?" Det. Becker asked, keeping a straight face.

"The last time I was in there was when I worked here. It's been locked ever since." Ethel said, looking over at Claudia, who was still amused by Det. Becker's inference that Ethel and Carl were lovers.

"How many times were you in Maggie's apartment?" Det. Becker asked.

"Only twice. Once when the spirits of Deborah, Bruce, and Susan were following us, and I ended up tripping over a stuffed animal and hurting my hip. And the second time was when they found . . . that knife," Ethel said. Her smiled faded as she looked down at the floorboards.

"Speaking of spirits," Det. Becker said, lowering his notepad. "Is it now your belief that Maggie will not be tormented by that . . .?"

"Demon, Detective," Ethel said, looking up. "The demon vampire, nurse Deborah, and doctor Hancock are now gone from this place.

Maggie should be feeling better, but we still have to prove her innocence."

"I thought you were saying a little girl named Susan Knight committed the murder. At the risk of sounding like a fool," Det. Becker said, rubbing the back of his neck. "Why didn't you do anything about her? Is she still around?"

"I'm not sure, but I think she left when Maggie was no longer in the building," Ethel said, puckering her mouth in thought. "I haven't sensed her or seen evidence of her since the police took Maggie away. She could be in purgatory or limbo. I don't know, but I don't think she's here anymore."

"Doctor Suharto said you have been harassing him," Det. Becker said, knowing the doctor was exaggerating when he spoke of Ethel's phone call.

Ethel shook her head. "That buffoon; I was only trying to see if he has something to do with that unusual knife. I'm sure he's the same Doctor Suharto that was in that letter."

"May I suggest that you leave the investigation to the police department," Det. Becker said. "Otherwise, I think he may accuse you of harassment and I'm sure you don't want to end up in court over that."

"Yes, Detective," Ethel said, nodding with a smile. "I was just trying to help Maggie."

Det. Becker reached inside his jacket and took out the buccal kit. "Do you mind submitting a voluntary cheek sample for DNA?"

Ethel raised her eyebrows. "Do you think I killed Mr. Zimmerman?"

"Doctor Suharto voluntarily submitted a sample and a sample from you would help with our investigation," Det. Becker said, sounding as though it was routine.

Ethel stopped rocking. "Sure, whatever you want, Detective. But I don't think it's necessary because now that Deborah and Bruce aren't around to whisper into people's ears, trying to manipulate their thoughts and actions, things should be cleared up soon."

SIXTEEN

NORA BELLA, MAGGIE'S literary agent for the Raven Ridge Mysteries, sat behind her Manhattan office desk relieved that the contract with Pendleton Books for Dane Slegers thriller series was officially finalized. Both Nora and Pendleton Books were optimistic about the success of his upcoming books, anticipating millions of dollars from them and the optioned movie deal.

It was a Tuesday afternoon and she debated whether to call it quits for the day and celebrate with her assistant, Yani, at Italia Cuisine and Cocktails across the street. First, she would straighten her desk and clear it of unnecessary stacks of papers, that way she could start fresh on the next contract in the morning. Unfortunately, she would be dealing with Pendleton Books, they wanted out of the contract with Maggie because she was not producing and was not satisfying the agreement, and that meant money lost.

"Damn it, Maggie," Nora said to herself as she stood. "Why did you have to go all nuts on me?"

She lifted the first stack of manuscripts and took them out to Yani, setting the pile on the corner of her desk. "Can you sort through these and organize them?" Nora began to walk away, then stopped and turned toward Yani. "Then we'll go next door and have cocktails in celebration of our success today."

Yani looked at the disheveled papers. "I can't believe you manage to get anything done. It looks like this paperwork was shuffled by a whirlwind before it decided to play a game of fifty-two pick up."

Nora laughed and began walking back to her office. She stopped when she noticed an envelope on the shiny marble floor. She picked it up. It was the letter Maggie had sent her a back in June, back before she went to the loony bin. She took it back to her office and sat at her desk. "I suppose it's about time I open this."

She opened the letter and began reading:

"Dear Nora,

It is June 13 and I'm writing you this letter because I trust you. Recently I've found out that my best friend, Jessica Pinter, had been having an affair with my husband. And I discovered that our will was altered and that valuable jewelry from our safe was missing, including the gun.

This may sound crazy, but I'm being made to look crazy, like I need psychiatric help, but I'm as sane as anyone. There are predators pursuing me, wanting to harm me.

Unfortunately, I'm also having weird dreams, like I'm somebody else from another time. In the dreams, I'm a nurse in this very same building when it was Lake Shore Sanatorium and Psychiatric Hospital; back in 1969. During that time, I was setup by a nurse named Deborah and a Dr. Hancock for the death of a young girl, who was a patient in the hospital. But I did not cause her death. In a strange turn of events, all three of us ended up dying in a boat explosion out on Lake Michigan. I don't believe in reincarnation, but there are so many coincidences it almost seems to be true.

I don't have the evidence I need to defend myself. When I get the evidence I need, I will move out of Sandpiper Bluff.

Please don't think I'm crazy. I'm being pursued and I don't know where to turn. But I wanted to write this as a record of my side of the story, and I trust you.

CONNIE MYRES

Your friend,

Maggie."

Nora was flipping her pen so quickly between her fingers that it flew across the room.

"Oh ... my ... god," Nora said, running out to Yani. The clicks of her high-heeled shoes, on the marble floor, echoed through the reception area. She put the paper on top of the disarrayed stack that Yani was already sorting. "Read this."

"What's wrong?" Yani said, picking up the letter.

"It's from Maggie McGee, read it." Nora watched Yani unfold the paper and begin reading.

When Yani had finished, she looked up in shock. "It was dated three months ago. You just now opened it?"

Nora shushed Yani's comment with her hands as if she could divert the words floating through the air. "We have to do something."

"You should call the police," Yani said, handing the letter back to Nora.

"What police? I don't know who to call," Nora said, pacing in the reception area.

"I'll look it up. It should be the police department where she lives." Yani looked up Maggie's address and then got on the Internet. "I'll dial the Black Water Police Department; they should be able to help."

"Do it," Nora said, clenching the letter.

Yani dialed the number and handed Nora the telephone receiver.

"Black Water Police Department, Deputy Clark speaking. How may I help you?"

"My name is Nora Bella and I'm a friend of Margaret McGee, actually I'm her literary agent here in Manhattan and I have come across some relevant information regarding her. Did I call the right place?"

"I believe Detective John Becker in homicide is handling her case," Dep. Clark said. "I'll transfer you over."

Moments later a female answered the phone. "Homicide, this is Detective Wanat. What can I do for you?"

"I need Detective Becker; I believe he's following Margaret McGee's case. Is he there?"

"You're in luck, he just walked in. What did you say your name was?"

"Nora Bella, Maggie's friend and agent," she said, speaking quickly.

"Johnny, you have a call from a Nora Bella, she said she's a friend of Margaret McGee's. I'll transfer her over," Det. Wanat said.

Det. Becker picked up the phone. "Detective John Becker."

Nora's words were rushed. "My name is Nora Bella and I just found a letter that Maggie McGee sent me back in June and I . . . well . . . just now opened it. It sounds like people were out to get her and . . . I think you had better read it. I'll overnight it to you."

"Do you have the envelope it was mailed in?" Det. Becker asked.

"I do, and I'll send that, too," Nora said. "I feel so bad for just now opening the letter, but I hope it helps her. I'm overnighting it right now."

After a short conversation with the detective, Nora hung up and handed the letter to Yani. "Overnight this immediately. And forget about that pile of papers, we're going for that cocktail right now."

SEVENTEEN

"I HAVEN'T BEEN home in two days," Claudia said, wiping her eyeglasses with a tissue. "My neighbors are going to think I'm in the hospital or have checked into a nursing home."

Ethel looked out her living room window. Another day had dawned and the birds were singing, the sun was shining, and there was not a raven or an approaching fog bank in sight. "Things are still good today."

"When were you going to check that video camera?" Claudia asked, putting on her glasses.

"I'll check it right now," Ethel said, keeping the curtains closed. She had not gotten around to cleaning the red letters from her front window. "I'll be right back."

Ethel walked out of her apartment and past the broken glass that was now scattered across the lobby floor from the building shaking

CONNIE MYRES

yesterday. She walked to the stairs and flipped on the light switch. The basement lights flicked on. Good, no need for a flashlight.

She walked down the steps and into the hallway. The foundation had shifted and it seemed that if she made too much noise, the vibration alone would topple the old hospital, or at least the east wall onto her, burying her in a heap of rubble. Tim Chandler would surely condemn the place and request that she move out immediately.

Ethel found the crevice where she had put the video camera to record a section of the basement, especially the scrying room. She reached up to retrieve the camera, but it was stuck. The shifting of the building had caused the crevice to collapse onto the camcorder. Not only that, but the basement floor was wet, likely from a fractured water pipe, she thought.

Then she smelled oil or gas, probably from the furnace and another broken pipe. It occurred to her that the building could be a ticking time-bomb, ready to explode with the flick of a match or click of an electrical switch. She knew, or at least was pretty sure, that Det. Becker had called Tim and told him about the building shaking and that he needed to have it inspected, but he had not been out yet, at least as far as she knew. However, she knew that she and Claudia needed to get out of the building, but not until she got the camera.

"Damn it," Ethel said, wiggling the camera side-to-side.

She looked around for something she could use to chip away at the broken concrete. The only thing she saw was a piece of steel rebar that had become dislodged from the building's shaking. She began chipping away at the old stone concrete until she was finally able to joggle the camera enough to get it out.

She looked toward the scrying room and around the basement. This would be her last time down here. Sadness overtook her as memories of the place, from when she worked there in the nineteen sixties as the primary receptionist, brought tears to her eyes. She envisioned kitchen staff preparing food for the patients, nurses in the locker room, and Mr. Zimmerman retrieving his broom from the janitor's closet. She smiled; oh, how he was fun to speak with. When he swept the lobby, he always had a joke for her. He had a joke book, actually more than one, which was where he would get his daily jokes. She was fond of him back in his youth, before he had a beer belly, when he had a head full of hair. He was fond of her, too.

A loud pop in the wall next to her jarred her from reminiscing and made her run back to the staircase. She and Claudia would need to leave the building before it was too late. She moved quickly to her apartment, ignoring her aching hip.

"Claudia, we need to get out of here," Ethel said, limping toward her purse and the golden box.

"Why?" Claudia said, looking up from a Dean Koontz book. "I just got comfortable."

"This place is ready to explode," Ethel said, not bothering to close the apartment door.

"Explode? Do you think you can get any more dramatic?" Claudia said, scooting forward on the sofa so that she could get the leverage she needed to stand.

"I'm not joking," Ethel said, going into her bedroom. She took an old hard-sided suitcase from her closet and began stuffing it with clothes, a picture of a youthful her and Mr. Zimmerman holding hands on the beach, spell books from her bookshelf, and her unique tea blend of elderflowers and black tea leaves.

"What do you want me to do?" Claudia asked, finally standing.

"I'll help you put on Maggie's backpack and then let's get out of here," Ethel said, barely able to lift the wheelless ancient luggage.

There was a loud crack and the floor shook. Ethel and Claudia left the apartment so fast; it was as if Deborah and Bruce were chasing them down the hallway. The old chandelier in the lobby ceiling began swinging, as the building shifted, just like the floor of a carnival's haunted house. They rushed into the vestibule and then out the front door onto the porch. The entry began collapsing around them as they ran, and yes, they ran, down the steps to Ethel's old gray sedan.

"Get in," Ethel said, putting the suitcase and magic box into the back seat.

Claudia miraculously slid out of the backpack and threw it in the backseat next to the suitcase. No sooner had Ethel started the car than the 1899 three-story building began collapsing. A plume of gray dust rushed over the car as bricks and wood scattered over the lawn, toward the parking lot.

Ethel clenched the steering wheel, closed her eyes, and braced for an impact. The sound of the old hospital collapsing was louder than she had expected. She opened her eyes as the dust cleared and she saw that half of the building was now a heap of broken timbers and plaster.

Claudia looked at Ethel. "I guess you're staying with me for a while."

"When we get to your place I'll call Tim and let him know that half of the demolition has already been done," Ethel said. She squirted window washer fluid on the windshield and turned on the wipers, smearing the soot over the glass. "I'm going to miss this place."

"I'm not," Claudia said, smacking her cane against the dashboard. "Let's go."

♀ ♀ ♀

ETHEL PULLED INTO the driveway of Claudia's small old-fashioned cottage. From the house foundation to the curb, weeds mingled with red hollyhocks, white hydrangeas, aromatic violet catmint, and any other wildflower that decided to take up residence. The cottage itself had shutters and a wood-shingled roof. Ethel noticed that Claudia had taken the time to fill the window boxes with Petunia and vines, only to let weeds share the bed.

The tiny home with its tiny yard was the perfect size for a single woman such as Claudia, well it used to be, Ethel thought. Seasonal freezing and thawing of the ground had upheaved the flagstone in the walkway leading to the front door.

"I'm glad I'm home," Claudia said, getting out of the car.

Ethel stepped out of the car and opened the door to the backseat. "It's been ages since I've been here. You used to have the quaintest cottage garden I have ever seen. It was just like a home in a fairy tale."

"Used to be is right," Claudia said, picking up Maggie's backpack.

Ethel pulled her suitcase and the magic box from the backseat and followed Claudia to the front door. The tip of her moccasin caught on the edge of a flagstone, causing her to trip. "If I fall and hurt my other hip, your next job may be that of a nursemaid."

"Dream on, Ethel," Claudia said, walking into her home. She sat the backpack on the floor beside the door. "Don't mind the mess, I wasn't expecting company."

Ethel looked around the interior. A fireplace and mantel took up most of the back wall, while a recliner, end table, sofa, china cabinet, and television set, took up the rest of the space. The décor was more American Craftsman than the Victorian style that Ethel preferred. The kitchen was small, containing only a sink, refrigerator, stove, and small dinette table. The only other rooms were a bathroom and a bedroom.

"There's only one bedroom, isn't there?" Ethel said.

Claudia nodded. "The davenport will serve you until you find another place to live."

Ethel sat her suitcase and magic box on the kitchen table. Then she unlatched the hard-sided suitcase and took out the video camera. She flipped open the viewing screen and turned on the power. "I'm dying to see what's on this."

Claudia walked up next to her and looked at the tiny picture. First, it showed Ethel placing the camera in its crevice and then walk to the scrying room. Because the scrying room door was open during the séance, it showed the whole thing. It showed two shadow people walk to the scrying room door and it showed the blackest of black shapes standing inside the room, next to the table. Unfortunately, because of the building shaking, most of the séance was a blur until the ritual ended and Det. Becker entered the room. Then it showed them pick up the crystal ball and leave.

"I'm showing this to the detective," Ethel said. "It is proof there are spirits."

Then it cut to a later time. A man was walking down the hall with a flashlight.

"That's Doctor Suharto," Ethel said, watching the screen intently.

She and Claudia watched as he went into the scrying room and over to the large oval mirror with intertwining and coiling snakes carved into the wooden frame. They watched as he took down the mirror and laid it face down on the table.

"What's he doing?" Claudia asked.

"It looks like he's removing the back," Ethel said. "That must be where he had the knife hidden all these years."

They heard the doctor cuss and then watched as he hung the mirror back on the wall.

"After I call Tim and let him know his apartment building is no longer standing, I'm driving to the police station and showing the detective this video," Ethel said. "Do you want to come along?"

"No way," Claudia said, opening a cabinet filled with liquor bottles. "I'm making me an Irish coffee, getting into my pajamas, and reading Odd Thomas. Are you coming back here when you're done?"

"Where else do I have to go?" Ethel said, limping out the door with the camera.

EIGHTEEN

"DETECTIVE BECKER, THE preliminary DNA results on the karambit are in," Peggy said, walking up to the detective's desk. "It's not final, but you may be surprised by what the results have returned."

Det. Becker took the sheet of paper from her hand.

"What's it say, Johnny?" Det. Wanat asked, looking eagerly at his expression.

He read some more and then said, "Ms. McGee's and Mr. Zimmerman's DNA was confirmed, but we already knew it would be. It says there were four that were either highly degraded, present in trace amounts or comprised of impurities. However, one of the samples did show degraded blood."

"Probably from that orderly that was murdered in 1969," Det. Wanat said, nodding.

CONNIE MYRES

"You were thinking this could be the same murder weapon."

"Highly likely," Det. Becker said. He continued reading aloud, "Doctor Suharto's DNA sample did not come back with a match, but it says that there were no good samples to compare it to."

"What about the psychic's DNA," Det. Wanat said. "I think she looks like a suspect."

"It came back the same as the doctor's; the degraded DNA samples are too far gone."

"There's one more," Peggy said, pointing further down the list.

Det. Becker looked at the paper and shook his head. "There were three fresh DNA samples on the knife, we know two of them, but the third is unidentified; it didn't match Ms. Dory or Doctor Suharto."

"There's someone else involved," Peggy said. "Someone else has recently handled the karambit."

Det. Becker's phone rang.

"There's a Ms. Dory here to see you," the officer said on the other end of the line.

"Tell her I'll be right down," Det. Becker said. He hung up the phone and looked at Det. Wanat. "The psychic has something for me. I'll be right back."

Det. Becker met Ethel in the lobby of the police station. He was surprised at how haggard she looked. The green scarf tied around her head was lopsided; her colorful gypsy skirt looked like it had not been washed in days, and the skin on her face seemed to sag more than usual. What had not changed was her sandpapery voice.

"Detective, thank you for seeing me," Ethel said, walking toward him. "I have a video you may be interested in."

He watched her pull open the camera's screen. "What do you have?"

"Watch and you'll see," Ethel said, positioning the screen so that they both could view it. "This was recorded on the last day at the apartment building. You can tell by the date."

He watched as Ethel hit play and the video began. He recognized the basement and the scrying room. Then his jaw dropped and his eyes widened, he could not believe what he was seeing. There appeared to be two ghosts outside the scrying room and something tall and dark, moving inside the room next to Ethel and Claudia. He did not see these people—these things—when he was down there and there no way they could walk past him without him noticing. And he doubted Ethel, or Claudia, had the skills to fake the video. Especially when he saw the video of him walking down the hallway to the room. It was he, no doubt about it.

"There's more," Ethel said, wiggling her finger at the screen.

Then the video switched to a later time and another man entering the basement. He saw the man walk into the scrying room, take the mirror from the wall and open its back before replacing it on the wall. He did not recognize the man until he saw his face as he walked out of the room empty handed. It was Dr. Suharto.

"That's all there is," Ethel said. "What do you think? Do you believe me now when I talk about spirits? And what about the person who went into the room last night. Do you recognize him?"

Det. Becker ran a hand through his hair. "I don't know what to say. I am shocked. But I'm curious; who do you think the man was?"

"It was Doctor Suharto, no doubt about it," Ethel said, closing the screen. "I don't think he murdered Mr. Zimmerman, but I do think he had gone down in the basement to see if that . . . karambit . . . was still where he had hidden it decades ago. The weapon that killed an orderly."

The man looked like Dr. Suharto and he obviously had some reason for going into the basement and looking for something. Whatever he was looking for was gone because he walked out with nothing in his hands. It was becoming apparent that this was the same Dr. Suharto that same doctor written about in the letter from Dr. Hancock to a nurse named Deborah Franklin. "Do you mind if I keep this camera?"

Ethel handed the camera to him. "Sure, you can have it. It belongs to Maggie, I just borrowed it."

"I am curious, though," Det. Becker said, taking it from her. "Why would Doctor Suharto suddenly decide that he should check for the karambit, and how did he enter the building?"

Ethel smiled sheepishly. "Well, I may have suggested to him that the building was going to be torn down and I may have . . . left the front door unlocked."

Det. Becker did not say anything. He knew Ethel had baited the doctor and the doctor took the bait. He smiled. "Is there anything else?"

"I'm staying with Claudia. I gave the phone number and address to the police officer at the window," Ethel said, turning to smile at the clean-cut young man.

"Thank you," Det. Becker said.

"Oh, one more thing," Ethel said. "Maggie goes to court tomorrow and I was wondering if you have gotten any closer to finding out who the murderer is?" Ethel asked.

"We're still working on it," Det. Becker said.

Ethel gave a reluctant nod and turned toward the door. He watched her as she moved hunched over and then limp out of the building. Whoever matched the other fresh DNA sample was likely the murderer. But who did it belong to?

"Johnny," said the police officer at the lobby window. "This just came in for you. It's addressed as urgent."

Det. Becker walked to the window. The officer handed him the letter that Nora Bella had overnighted to him. He took it back to his office and opened it. Maggie was appearing less guilty, but there was no concrete evidence to clear her.

NINETEEN

MAGGIE SAT WITH her hands handcuffed behind her back and her ankles in shackles, in the backseat of the police station's van. She was being driven from Port Glenn Psychiatric and Forensic Hospital to the Black Water courthouse for a preliminary hearing. Now that she was found competent to stand trial she knew that this, trial before the trial, would bring evidence before the court showing there was due cause to continue on to the felony criminal trial.

Oddly, she felt better today than at any time since this all started. She woke up refreshed, not tired and depleted of energy like she usually was. Even the two nodules on her neck, while still there, felt smaller and less tender. And even though she had only spoken with her court-appointed attorney one time, and that was over the phone, she felt better able to handle whatever decision was made.

As the van barreled down the highway, she looked out the side window and watched cornfields and farms whiz by. Oh, how she wished she were in one of those houses, in one of those yards, or any other place than in the van driving her to whatever fate that lay ahead.

She knew the court would find probable cause and she would be bound over to trial court. Unless Ethel could work her magic, she would be imprisoned.

TWENTY

JESS WOKE UP with a pounding headache. Rather than blowing her brains out three days ago, she ended up drinking herself to oblivion. She held her throbbing head as she sat up. Her clothes were wet from spilled alcohol, gin bottles and beer cans were all over the place, and Cory's handgun still sat on the coffee table. For a moment, she thought that a bullet to the head would be less painful than the way she was feeling at that moment.

When she sat on the edge of the couch, she put her foot in something wet. It was vomit. The place smelled of vomit. She wiped her food on a dry patch of the carpet and went into the kitchen where a bottle of aspirin sat already open on the counter. It was empty.

"Damn," she said, tossing it into the sink with dirty dishes.

She opened the refrigerator for something cold to drink, but there was nothing. She must have drunk everything all ready. As she closed the refrigerator door, images began flashing through her mind. Confusing images. Bad images.

She stumbled to the kitchen table, sat down, and put her elbows on the table so that she could hold her head. The images seemed fresh and seemed real. She remembered leaving Maggie's apartment after she spent the night, and she remembered the voices, voices in her ear, telling her to go to the basement and to take a knife from behind a mirror. She remembered doing as the voice said, and she took a knife, wrapped in a stained cloth, from behind the mirror. She saw the odd mirror with the writhing snakes, and she saw herself removing the back to take out the knife and then replacing the mirror. She remembered the mirror being heavy and she remembered the voices, male and female, telling her exactly what to do as if she were in a trance.

Tears streamed down her eyes as she remembered finding a skeleton key, just like Maggie's, in a drawer in the storage room, along with a roll of binder twine. She remembered going back to Sandpiper Bluff and going into Maggie's apartment, when she was not home, and taking the sunglasses. Then she remembered climbing the stairs to the third floor and knocking on Mr. Zimmerman's door. The fool was drunk and let her in. When he saw the knife she was wielding, he went to the bedroom as she instructed and laid face down. She remembered him pleading to not hurt him. He sobbed, saying he would do whatever she wanted. But she tied all four limbs to the legs of his bed, with the binder twine, just like the voices told her a patient had once been restrained. What she wanted was to hack him to death, and that was exactly what she did.

Jess saw herself murdering Mr. Zimmerman as the man cried out for her to stop. His cries were sickening and pitiful. Then, as the voices instructed, she left the sunglasses that Maggie had borrowed from her.

Jess saw herself leaving the bedroom with the bloody knife and walking by the TV dinner he had been eating. She took a French fry from the tray, ate it, and left.

Jess screamed and pounded the table with her fist, causing a saltshaker to topple over and roll to the floor. The images were not over. She then saw herself going back and hacking away at the superintendent on other nights. The voices in her head became louder and the images became vivid and real after the murder. She was able to see a little girl, and a man and a woman. They talked to her vile talk, mixed with words of rewards for doing their dirty work. They enticed her to join them in their ecstasy.

The man, who called himself Bruce, would come to her at night like an incubus, and lie upon her as she slept. And the woman, who called herself Deborah, would tell her how she was prettier and better than Maggie. That Maggie had to pay the price for interfering with their eternal lust. And they told her that she, Jess, could join them and never want for anything.

Jess wiped her eyes and began pulling her hair. The memories were clear and they were real. It was then that she realized that it was she who had committed the crime.

"Why did I do it?" Jess yelled, not caring if anyone could hear her psychic breakdown through the thin trailer walls. "It was those damned voices. They made me do it."

Then she remembered that Maggie's court date was today. She picked up her purse and ran to her car, not even bothering to close the trailer's door. She looked and felt like shit.

When she got to the courthouse, she ran up to a window. "What court room is Maggie McGee in?"

The clerk looked shocked by Jess's appearance and then said. "Courtroom 222."

Jess ran up the elegant round staircase and to the courtroom door. She knew that if she went in and confessed, her life was over. But she loved Maggie and shame overtook her. She went into the courtroom, reeking of alcohol and vomit.

She saw Maggie in handcuffs sitting at the defendant's table with her attorney.

As Maggie turned her head to see who had come in through the door, and as a guard approached her, she shouted, "I did it. I killed Mr. Zimmerman. Maggie is innocent."

Jess saw a gypsy woman stand up in the gallery and bring her hands to her face in disbelief and relief. She heard the judge pound his gavel as the spectators chattered. Then she saw Maggie, her dear friend Maggie, look at her with love. Jess knew she had done the right thing. Love conquers all.

1 Peter 4:8. Above all, preserve an intense love for each other, since love covers over many a sin.

The End

Thank you for reading!

ConnieMyres.com

IRISH COFFEE

Ingredients

- 1 cup freshly brewed hot coffee
- 1 tablespoon brown sugar (or 2 oz. Baileys Original Irish Cream)
- 1 jigger Irish whiskey (1 ½ ounces or 3 tablespoons)
- Heavy cream, slightly whipped

Directions

1. Fill a mug with hot water to preheat it, and then empty.
2. Pour piping hot coffee into warmed mug until it is about ¾ full.
3. Add the brown sugar (or Baileys Original Irish Cream) and stir until completely dissolved.
4. Blend in Irish whiskey.
5. Top with a collar of the whipped heavy cream by pouring gently over the back of a spoon.
6. Serve hot.

1 fluid ounce = 2 tablespoons

*Claudia made Irish coffee in chapter 17.

RECOMMENDED BOOK

Raven's Ridge: A Haunted Mystery

Ghost, Thrillers, Suspense, Supernatural, Mystery and Detective, Crime

Mental illness can cause hallucinations; so how can you determine a delusion from the real thing?

Rose Compton moved into her family's old lumber baron mansion, looming near the edge of a Lake Michigan cliff. She loves her adult children and will do anything for them, except move out of Raven's Ridge. Spooky and menacing events make her wonder if she is developing dementia, like her deceased mother, or if a ghost is haunting the estate.

Visit ConnieMyres.com

or

Books2Read.com/ConnieMyres

Also by Connie

STANDALONE BOOKS

Twisted Intentions, Beneath the White Veil, Ring, Haunting of Ender House, Rest Stop Terror, Solus, Who Killed Sweet Violet?, Lucifer's Island, Raven's Ridge

PACIE ROSE MYSTERIES

Pacie Rose Mysteries (Books 1–3)
Slenderman, Hornet, Wolf
Jezebel, My Name is Mr. Dibble

RANCOR

Rancor: A Paranormal Psychological Thriller (Books 1 & 2)
Sinister Attachments, Unrestrained

READ AS CONNIE WRITES

Three Sisters Odyssey

SEVEN SEALS REDUX

Seven Seals Redux: The Complete Apocalyptic Novel Series (Books 1–7)
White Horse, Red Horse, Black Horse, Pale Horse, Tribulation, Signs, Trumpets

SUSPENSE STORIES

Suspense Stories #1: Raven's Ridge, Lucifer's Island, Sinister Attachments

PUBLIC DOMAIN

The Secret of Chimneys by Agatha Christie

WATCH FOR SPOOKY SHORTS

Spooky Shorts A-G: A Collection of Creepy Short Stories
Apple Pie, Black-Eyed Kids, Creature, Dungeon, Electric, Fairy, Genie, House, Ice, Joker, Kiss, Lucid, Minion, Neighbor, Obelisk, Pattern, Quest, Rumor, Squatch, Time, Underwold, Visitor, Wolf, X-axis, Yellow, ZoZo

The complete list of books can be found at
ConnieMyres.com
or
Visit my Books2Read Author Page

CONNIE MYRES, a multi-genre author specializing in horror, mystery, suspense, and science fiction, has been spinning thrilling tales since her childhood in Michigan. From a young age, she captivated her audiences—children she babysat—by weaving them into her suspense-filled narratives, igniting an insatiable love for storytelling.

Inspired by the works of literary masters such as Dean Koontz and Stephen King, Connie has crafted her own unique style that keeps readers on the edge of their seats. Her vivid, dynamic stories, filled with intrigue and surprise, mirror her own multi-faceted life. Not only a talented writer, Connie is a registered nurse and a developer, showing her knack for both caring for others and creating immersive digital worlds.

In the future, Connie plans to join the digital nomad movement, allowing her love for adventure and new experiences to fuel her compelling narratives further. For now, she continues to captivate and inspire from her home base in Michigan, crafting stories that both engage and terrify her readers.

Stay connected with Connie through her website at ConnieMyres.com, where you can explore her wide range of books and short stories, and join her on this incredible storytelling journey.

FEATHER AND FERMION PUBLISHING

Feather and Fermion Publishing is a Michigan-based publisher that was founded in 2014. Our mission is to provide readers with thrilling and entertaining stories across a variety of genres, including horror, mystery, suspense, thriller, science fiction, and fantasy. We publish original fiction under our two imprints: Oort Cloud Books and White-Knuckle Books.

Author Connie Myres owns Feather and Fermion Publishing.

VISIT CONNIE'S WEBSITE

Visit Connie's website and find her books, blog, sales, and more.

ConnieMyres.com

CONNIE MYRES
AUTHOR